The Cape

And Other Stories
from the Japanese Ghetto

The Cape

And Other Stories
from the Japanese Ghetto

Kenji Nakagami

Translated, with a Preface and an Afterword,
by Eve Zimmerman

STONE BRIDGE FICTION
Stone Bridge Press
Berkeley, California

Published by
Stone Bridge Press, P.O. Box 8208, Berkeley, CA 94707
510-524-8732 • sbp@stonebridge.com • www.stonebridge.com

Except on the cover, title page, and this copyright page, names of Japanese persons throughout this work appear according to Japanese convention, that is, family name first.

Originally published in Japan as *Misaki* ("The Cape," 1975), *Kataku* ("House on Fire," 1975), and *Akagami* ("Red Hair," 1978).

Cover design by Linda Ronan.
Book design by Robert Goodman, Silvercat, San Diego, California.

© 1999 Stone Bridge Press. Stone Bridge Fiction edition published 2008.

Printed in the United States of America.

2013 2012 2011 2010 2009 2008   10 9 8 7 6 5 4 3 2 1

LIBRARY OF CONGRESS CATALOGING-IN-PUBLICATION DATA
Nakagami, Kenji.
    [Selections. English. c1999]
    The cape and other stories from the Japanese ghetto / Kenji
Nakagami: translated by Eve Zimmerman.
        p.   cm.
        Contents: Misaki (The cape)—Kataku (House on fire)—Akagami
(Red hair).
    ISBN 978-1-933330-43-3.
        1. Nakagami, Kenji—Translations into English.   I. Title.
PL857.A3683A28   1999
    895.6'35—dc21   99-12378
                                                      CIP

for Nori

Contents

Translator's Preface

Shingū (pop. 35,000) is a wet place. Located at the foot of high mountains on the Kii Peninsula near the southernmost tip of central Honshu, it is subject to dramatic turns of weather. The rain falls so hard that people say it rains from the ground up. Sitting in a coffee shop one Sunday in May during the rainy season, Matsumoto Iwao, a local sake dealer, speaks about Shingū's unique history: its natural wealth in coal, paper, and lumber; its oppression by the central government (a number of Shingū locals were persecuted in the Great Treason Incident of 1910); and its eventual marginalization when it was divided between Wakayama and Mie prefectures (it was situated in the province of Kii, or Kishū). Recalling Shingū's more prosperous days, Matsumoto describes a feeling of separatism on the part of Shingū people, who still nurse resentment toward the center.

The talk soon turns to the writer Nakagami Kenji (1946–92), Matsumoto's school friend who enjoyed meteoric success in Tokyo and returned home to die of kidney cancer at the age of forty-six. Matsumoto, a frail child, had been picked on by the other children, and the young Kenji, large for his age, walked him home from school. There was a certain irony to this relationship. It was Nakagami, not Matsumoto, who was born into the outcastes'

(*burakumin*) community of Shingū and who, according to Matsumoto, was at times made to feel unwelcome in the homes of their
school friends. But the young Kenji took on the role of protector.

Not far from where we are sitting is the old site of the outcaste neighborhood, the network of alleyways that once wound
out from the back of the train station—the *roji* or "alleyway" as
it is called in Nakagami's fiction. According to one aging former occupant of the alleyways, now ill in the People's Hospital
of Shingū, the outcastes suffered severe poverty and discrimination before World War II. Those who lived along the alleyways
did not often venture into the town, knowing that they would
be ignored or openly ostracized. For the most part, the outcastes
had very little formal schooling and soon entered the distinctive
"unclean" trades of slaughterer, shoe mender, and day laborer.
When times grew hard it was not uncommon for a woman to
be sold to a brothel for a time to put food on the table, and my
informant remembered a number of such cases. When it was time
to marry, the people from the alleyway would choose partners
from a pool of other outcastes who lived in communities scattered
along the southern Kishū coast.[1]

Since outcastes are racially and ethnically identical to other
Japanese, the origins of their status are still shrouded in mystery
and seem to vary from place to place. Most historians trace the
creation of a rigid outcaste class back to the early eighteenth cen-
tury when the Tokugawa government issued a number of edicts
defining outcaste status and listing rules to regulate outcaste
dress, freedom of movement, and even the style of houses they
could build (there could be no windows facing the street). These
edicts coincided with a time when craftspeople working with
leather had gathered in the castle towns to provide weaponry

---

[1] Personal interview with Matsune Hisao, Shingū, July 1993.

for the new military class. Some scholars assert more ancient origins, discovering evidence of settled outcasts communities in the fourteenth and fifteenth centuries.[2] These conflicting theories notwithstanding, Ian Neary traces a development over time in the formation of outcaste identity: "Whereas before 1600 the emphasis was on occupation afterwards it was on bloodline, but why this should be has not been clearly explained."[3] At least one theory has been debunked—that the outcastes are not Japanese but the descendants of Koreans or ancient slaves.[4]

In the early 1970s, the Japanese government, unable to ignore the widening gap in living standards between outcastes and prosperous middle-class Japanese, began to throw money at the outcaste problem. Nakagami's neighborhood in Shingū was the beneficiary: the old alleyways were bulldozed and replaced with concrete prefab buildings, a hill that separated the neighborhood from the town was razed, and a department store was built nearby. Nakagami's relatives and others profited from the change: they received construction contracts or jobs, and many moved away. Much of Nakagami's fiction traces the conflict, corruption, and even violence that marked this project of urban renewal.

Although the present-day outcaste neighborhood is but a shadow of its former self, a time when the people huddled together defensively, their doors open to each other, their children wandering back and forth,[5] there are still markers in 1998. Across from the Shingū city hall a banner reads, "Let's get rid of all discrimination, starting with discrimination against the *burakumin*." There are many shoe stores near the station, a leftover from the

---

[2] See Ian Neary, "Burakumin in Contemporary Japan," *Japan's Minorities*, ed. Michael Weiner (London: Routledge, 1997), pp. 52–55.

[3] Ibid., p. 55.

[4] Ibid., p. 52.

[5] Nakagami discussed the communal aspects (*kyōdōtaisei*) of life in the *roji* in a personal interview in 1989 in New York City.

days when the outcastes mended *geta* (clogs) and worked with leather, and when I enter one and show my map to ask directions, I immediately realize that the proprietor cannot read. There are also the family names—fully recognizable to the people of the town—revealing who was born in the *roji*. Discrimination still rears its head when people marry.

Nakagami Kenji was born in 1946 in the alleyway in Kasuga-chō next to the railroad tracks on the site of what is currently government-issued prefab building #13. The spot is now marked on tourist maps of Shingū, the city that also claims Nakagami as its own on a large billboard by the station. By returning home as a famous writer, Nakagami literally put what was once invisible on the map. Yomota Inuhiko, a critic and friend of Nakagami's, charges that the worst aspect of discrimination against the outcastes is the secrecy that attends its practice.[6] Through his writing, his regular visits to Shingū, and his enthusiastic embrace of his own people and their past, Nakagami broke this secrecy and brought the dark, impenetrable network of alleyways into the light. As the old survivor of the alleyway said succinctly: "Nakagami made me proud to be *burakumin* for the first time in my life."

Reading Nakagami

Nakagami's fiction poses certain challenges to the reader: a layered narrative structure that switches between time periods and points of view and a complex cast of characters. "The Cape" and

---

[6] Personal interview with Yomota Inuhiko, Tokyo, June 1998.

"House on Fire" share many of the same characters—the father, the elder brother, the mother, even the main character (the son in "House on Fire" is simply an older version of Akiyuki). Both stories also share certain events and take place in the same location (although the grown son lives in Tokyo). The genealogical chart on page xiv will simplify both stories. "Red Hair," with only two main characters and a simple narrative, stands alone.

Acknowledgments

Thanks to all who made this translation possible—readers, teachers, detectives, and babysitters: Paul Anderer, Rachel Belash, Peter Goodman, Hosea Hirata, Erin Hurney, Seth Lloyd, Shawn Maurer, Morimoto Yūji, the Nakagami family, Kazuko Oliver, Yuiko Yampolsky, the Yomotas, and all my seminar students.

Family Relationships in "The Cape" (and "House on Fire")

This chart provides a simplified layout of the relationships of the characters in "The Cape." Later Nakagami works encompass additional family members and interconnections. The chart also illustrates the primary relationships in "House on Fire," where the father character is named Yasu.

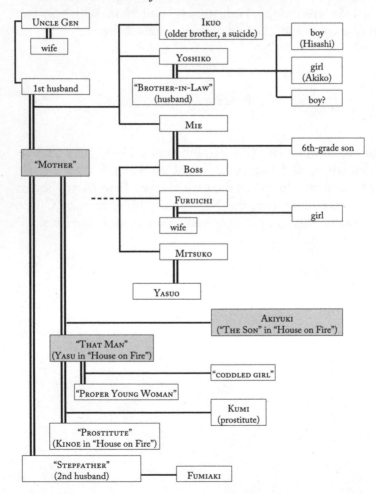

The Cape

The night insects were just beginning to hum. If he listened hard he could hear them far away, like a buzzing in his ears. All night long, the insects would hum. Akiyuki imagined the smell of the cold night earth.

His sister came in with a large plate of meat.

"Hey, how 'bout a drink?" Kan asked her, holding up a beer bottle.

"I don't drink," said Mie. She set the plate down beside the charcoal grill. "I'm scared to. We've got this thing in our blood. It kills our brains. Just the sight of *him* drinking worries me," she spoke intently, looking not at Kan but at Akiyuki, his face red from a single glass of beer, his big body hunched over, his breath hot.

She smiled, on the verge of tears.

Kan didn't intend to press the sister to drink. He just wanted to thank her for supplying him and the other workers with beer and meat.

"Oh, have a drink," slurred Mitsuko from across the table, "Forget the boss every once in a while and live it up."

"I can't. I can't." Mie, smiling, shook her head.

"C'mon, go for it." Mitsuko shifted into a cross-legged position. Akiyuki could see her frilly peach underpants.

"Hey, cover yourself up, you," laughed Mitsuko's husband,

Yasuo. Seated next to her, he was now tugging at the skirt that had risen up over her knees.

"There's still plenty left for you. Who cares if I show it off a little?" Mitsuko pushed Yasuo away. "Let me tell you, Yasuo, I'm not like Mie here. I've been around a little. More than a little."

Mie collected the empty beer bottles and went back to the kitchen.

The front door and the windows of the house were open. After work the men had started drinking in the six mat office with the wooden floor where the boss had his desk. Curious, the neighborhood kids peeped in. The men sat in a semi-circle facing out onto the alleyway. A breeze sweeping down the alley carried away the odors of cooking meat, the iron and the dust from the boss's house. The air became suffused with the cold smells of the flowerpots tended by the old people and widows, and of the ditches and the quickly gathering night.

"Drink up, drink up, drink up. Who cares if we're short on brains?" said Yasuo, hoisting the beer bottle.

"Yeah, nobody here had much to begin with anyway." Akiyuki drained his glass. Yasuo poured him another.

"Well, my family's famous for its stupidity," said Mitsuko. The chopsticks she was using to turn the meat burst into flames. "My brother'll kill me for saying so, but it's true." She stuck out her tongue.

"The boss is no dummy. He's got brains," said Fujino.

"That's what you think. You say he's smart because he's your boss, but he's my flesh and blood. My second oldest brother, if you want to get picky about it. But when we were growing up I always thought he was an idiot. And who would know better than me?"

Mie yelled in from the kitchen. "Hey, stop badmouthing my old man!"

Mitsuko stuck out her tongue again.

"But no matter what anybody says," said Mitsuko, turning to Yasuo and rapping him on the head, "you come from the biggest line of idiots. You're even worse than I am. Wasn't it your grandfather who slept with some lousy whore and got the clap? And your father was the result, right?"

Yasuo gave a deep belly laugh. He showed no sign of being affected by the beer. A sober Yasuo was as docile as a cat. He was cheerful. He worked hard. He let Mitsuko poke fun at him. But a drunken Yasuo was another story.

Hearing Mie call, Akiyuki went to the kitchen.

"How about if you stop drinking now and take me to Mother's house? The road's scary at night."

"What are you going to do there?" Akiyuki asked. Even his voice felt hot from the alcohol.

"The memorial service, for Daddy," said Mie, "I need you for my bodyguard. Once they get a look at you, nobody'll bother us."

"Mie, you are such a chicken," Mitsuko chimed in from the office. "You could never live at the beach house."

Mitsuko turned to the others and started telling them what a coward Mie was. The beach house had been owned by Mitsuko's father. Sometime after the father's death, the oldest son, Furuichi, who worked for a trucking company, had moved in with his wife. Mitsuko often berated them for it. "I'm Daddy's girl. He meant for me to live in the beach house," she would say. The house was near the concrete embankments on the beach. Close by was a forest planted as a windbreak and a communal graveyard.

"What are you talking about? Is that your idea of being a chicken?" Mie quickly took Akiyuki by the hand. "Let's go, bodyguard. I'll be back soon. Mit-chan, make sure everybody has drinks while I'm gone."

"Chiiiiickennnnn," said Mitsuko. "But that's what makes her so adorable. She's not all in your face like Furuichi and his wife.

Next time the boss cheats on her, I'm gonna string him up."
Mitsuko leaned her head on Yasuo's shoulder.

The night air was cold. Akiyuki and Mie walked through the
alleyway, away from the railroad crossing. Mie took little running steps. She only came up to her brother's shoulder. Akiyuki
wrapped his jacket around his waist. The sweat in his cotton
undershirt suddenly chilled and felt good on his skin. Benches
holding potted plants were set out in the alleyway, and the aroma
of flowers filled the air. They followed the curve of the alleyway,
cut across a street that ran past the station, and walked down a
path through the fields. Again, the night insects sounded like a
buzzing in Akiyuki's ears. Taking a road that cut over the hill, the
two passed a cattle shed.

"Everybody's coming to Daddy's memorial service again," said
Mie. Then, out of the blue she spoke his name. "Akiyuki?"

He grunted.

"Don't flirt with Mitsuko. It upsets me. It could cause big
problems in the family."

"I understand," he said. With every step, his work breeches
rubbed together. He walked with his legs apart. His split-toed
cloth tabi shoes made no sound. A small car approached, its lights
blinding. In the moment they stood still and waited for the car to
pass, Mie looked over at her brother. A sweet scent of gasoline
washed over them.

"Akiyuki," said Mie, "hold my hand."

She took his hand in hers.

"What a baby," he said shaking her off. "Hey, chicken, you
scared?"

Mie took his hand again.

"I just now had this feeling you were…Akiyuki, hold my hand
like Brother used to. We always used to walk along this road
holding hands on our way to Mother's house. And when we got to

about here, he'd say, 'Mie, are you scared?' even though I was fine. But then I'd get scared because he asked me if I was."

Mie laughed softly. Her hand was cold and firm.

"Are things going O.K. with the boss?"

"Mmm," Akiyuki nodded.

"He can be harsh sometimes," said Mie.

Akiyuki had nothing to say.

It was barely a ten-minute walk from Mie and the boss's house. The mother was in the kitchen washing dishes. "You came at just the right time," she said, catching sight of Mie and drying her hands on a towel as she came to the door.

"I just had a call from Nagoya," scowled the mother. "It was Yoshiko, giving me a hard time again. 'But I'm the eldest daughter,' she says in her big know-it-all way."

"Where's Father?" asked Mie.

"Gone to a meeting. Fumiaki went back to his apartment." Seeing Akiyuki, she added, "Akiyuki, hurry up and eat your supper, then take a bath. I left a change of clothes in there for you." Then, as if she had just noticed his red face, she continued, "Drinking with the crew again? Don't blame me if you ache all over tomorrow."

"He just had one or two," said his sister, covering for him.

"Just a couple after work," Akiyuki said.

"Ah, well then, if it's just one or two," laughed the mother. "You're twenty-four, not fifteen or sixteen, so it's no big deal."

"He's just Brother's age when he died," said Mie, scrutinizing him.

"You're right," said the mother as she sat down at the low tea table. Suddenly her strength seemed to leave her. Mie's eyes shone in the glow of the fluorescent lamp.

"On our way here a couple minutes ago, I felt Brother was with me. It was spooky." Mie sat down. "He's really come to look like him."

"You're right," said the mother. "I think the same thing whenever I see him."

Akiyuki ate supper listening to the women talk. They were discussing the father's memorial service. On the phone a few moments before, Yoshiko, who lived in Nagoya, had been complaining that it was strange to hold a memorial service for her father in the stepfather's house. Akiyuki wasn't related by blood to either the father or the stepfather. His only tie to his siblings was through the mother. His real father was a man who wore workman's breeches and sunglasses, even though he didn't work in construction. A man with the snout of a lion and the body of a giant. Whenever his mother and sisters used the word "father," Akiyuki thought about the man. Every once in a while, he ran into him in town. The man spoke to him. They exchanged one or two words. And that was it. The man's face and body resembled his own. But what the hell did that mean? He'd heard a rumor—supposedly, the man was keeping some young woman in the red-light district. But Mie said the woman must be Akiyuki's half-sister by a different mother. Among all the man's children born to different women at just around the same time, she would be the daughter of the whore. Then after she'd grown up she'd come to the red-light district. Overnight the man had gotten rich. There were rumors that he'd swindled mountain property and other land out of a landowner. Every time Akiyuki thought of the man, he remembered what someone had once said: "There are terrible people in this world."

The women were still talking when Akiyuki finished his supper. As he entered the bathroom, the discussion showed no sign of ending. His body felt gritty from the dust. From the waist down, his skin was milky white. From the waist up, he was black from the sun. He doused himself with hot water.

৳

Akiyuki lived in a four-and-a-half-mat room separated from the rest of the house. On one wall was a poster of an actress. That was it. His friends had stereos, their own televisions, even sideboards in their rooms. If he wanted to he could easily buy such things with the salary he got twice a month from the boss. But he wasn't the type to decorate or buy furniture. In high school he'd been the same. When he graduated and went to work for the construction company in Osaka for six months, he'd kept nothing in his dorm room but a futon, underwear, and some work clothes. His dormmates eyed him suspiciously. He went to bed in his room and woke up in his room. It was the same now. And women? They didn't even cross his mind. He would remove all impurities. Come home from a hard day's work, take a bath, eat supper, go to sleep. Get up the next morning, wash your face, have breakfast. In the morning when the sun shone in, or as long as it wasn't raining, Akiyuki would put on a cotton shirt, his work breeches, and his split-toed tabi shoes. Every day he did the same.

The sun was beating down. In the main part of the house Akiyuki's stepfather and Fumiaki, the stepfather's son, were eating breakfast.

"What site are you on now?" asked Fumiaki.

Akiyuki didn't answer. Instead he did twenty push-ups and twenty sit-ups in his underwear. Then, still breathing hard, he washed his face in the sink next to the bathroom. His mother looked on.

"Did you pour concrete yet?"

"We're digging," he answered. He dried himself with the towel. "How about your crew?"

The stepfather didn't answer. Fumiaki responded instead. "We pour concrete today. If we don't work our asses off and finish it up, we'll fall behind. The weather looks good, too. We went to all that trouble bailing out the water, and we'll just have to do it over again if it rains."

Fumiaki's mouth puckered as he crunched on some pickles. Akiyuki's mother appeared from the room that had the Buddhist family altar. She was carrying clean breeches.

"The tabi are on the new side. I washed them, so wear them," she said testily.

The stepfather was sitting cross-legged in his work clothes, drinking tea. Streaks of gray in his hair rounded out the shape of his face. When had the gray hair become noticeable? In fact, when had his whole being become softer and kinder? It was a mystery to Akiyuki. He couldn't remember exactly when it had all started. It must have been around the time he and Fumiaki got into an argument at the concrete works. Relations became strained, so Akiyuki had quit his stepfather's crew to go work for his sister's husband's crew.

That day he wouldn't give in to Fumiaki, his stepfather had said, "You know he's two years older than you."

"I do know," was Akiyuki's answer.

The stepfather had just stared at him, without becoming angry. Back when Akiyuki had returned from his six-month stint with the construction company in Osaka and begun working for his stepfather, he and Fumiaki had occasionally got the back of a shovel. Fumiaki always got the worst of it. The stepfather would chase him around the yard.

"Don't bother coming back, you rotten shit," the stepfather would yell at Fumiaki as he fled. He wouldn't ever allow a child to speak back to him.

Sometimes, Akiyuki thought, he had a strange family. The four of them all lived together, the mother and her child, the father and his child. He and Fumiaki were stepbrothers, one without a mother, one without a father. But in fact, both of their absent parents were still alive. Fumiaki had been abandoned by his birth mother and didn't think of her as his mother, while Akiyuki didn't think of the man in town as his father. His sisters and his dead brother were the children of the mother's first husband. When his mother married his stepfather, she had brought him, the one who had a different father, along with her.

Akiyuki sat down next to Fumiaki and ate. His chest and arms were twice the size of Fumiaki's.

"Next time we get paid, let's go someplace fun," said Fumiaki, looking at his step-brother's naked torso. Akiyuki glanced over at his mother.

꿎

At the time Akiyuki got to the boss's house only two of the crew were there. He went and got the keys from his sister and opened the shed. It smelled of iron and coal.

Fujino, who commuted from one station away, quickly loaded a bamboo basket for carrying sand, a shovel, a bamboo scoop, and a pick into the back of a van.

"How about some hot tea?" asked Mie, poking her face out of the kitchen door. Her face looked puffy in the bright sunlight. The lone woman on the crew looked at Akiyuki for an answer.

"We'll have some," he replied.

The woman and Fujino sat down by the kitchen door to drink their tea while Akiyuki had his standing up outside. From inside came the voice of the boss: "We'll go in ten minutes.... Bunch of bums. You give 'em something to drink and they take the next day off!"

"They'll show up," said the woman.

"Not Yasuo. He's fucking up again."

The sound of the boss's voice made Akiyuki suddenly envision the sleepy couple embracing in the morning. He drained his tea. The light had reached them. The alley in front of the boss's house was bathed in sunshine. He could smell the ditches. There were no signs of life anywhere but here. Next to the railroad crossing, where the alleyway curved off to the left, a single tree was gently shaking its leaves. The tree reminded him of himself. Akiyuki didn't know what kind of tree it was, and he didn't care. The tree had no flowers or fruit. It spread its branches to the sun, it trembled in the wind. That's enough, he thought. The tree doesn't need flowers or fruit. It doesn't need a name. Suddenly, Akiyuki felt he was dreaming.

The sun was now just about to touch the roofs of the houses opposite. The boss and Mie's house was fully exposed. Akiyuki, leaning on the van, looked it over. What with one renovation after another, the house bore no resemblance to its former self. This was the house his brother had hanged himself in. But even the tree he had hanged himself on was gone now.

By six-thirty the only one who hadn't yet arrived was Yasuo. So on the way to the site they stopped at Yasuo and Mitsuko's apartment building, which had been built on land once used for farming. The boss sent Akiyuki up the stairs. "Tell them to get their shit together," the boss called after him. At Akiyuki's knock, a woman's voice answered: "Who is it?" Mitsuko poked her head out. When she saw it was Akiyuki, she laughed. "Oh, Aki-chan?" Her face looked pale and featureless, perhaps because she hadn't put on makeup yet.

"Hey, horndog, they're here to get you," Mitsuko called back into the room.

Mitsuko swung open the door. There was Yasuo, eating breakfast. Red curtains hung in the windows, and a stuffed toy dog sat on top of a sideboard. The futon was still out, its covers turned back and rumpled.

"Yasu, c'mon, don't drag your feet, get going," said Mitsuko.

"One more minute, one more minute," said Yasuo, stuffing his mouth.

"I'm the one who's going to get an earful from the boss again. Lazy horny bastard."

"Hey, look who's talking. Who's the horny one, eh, Akiyuki?" said Yasuo.

Akiyuki laughed uncomfortably.

Still smacking his lips, Yasuo finally got up and put on his work tabi. "You go back to sleep for all I care," he said, "but I'm going to work. I'm going to dig."

🜁

Akiyuki liked the feel of sweat on his naked skin. He drove the pick into the ground. Perhaps because the site was on a small rise on the mountains, the earth here was unusually soft, and the pick sank down deep into it. On the surface the ground was a cakey white. But underneath it was black with moisture. He began to shovel. The crew was putting in a drainage ditch. As soon as they finished digging, they immediately had to pour the concrete. In preparation for the job the gravel and sand for the concrete were already on the site.

"Aki-chan, one of these days let's go out somewhere."

"O.K.," Akiyuki responded to Yasuo.

Kan, along with the boss, was checking everything with a string and a measuring tape, referring constantly to the plans in order to prepare for pouring concrete the next day.

"If you go out with Yasuo, you're going to get stuck with his shit."

"What're you talking about?"

"First he chats them up in that soft-spoken voice, like he's some rich boy. Oh, he's good. No more drinks for me, he tells 'em. The women fall for it, but once he gets them outside he beats 'em up till they do whatever he wants. I wouldn't be caught dead with him. It's a miracle he hasn't been arrested."

"I have, twice," said Yasuo. He gave a great laugh.

The boss laughed back. "Teach Akiyuki any strange tricks and you'll have me to reckon with."

"Yes, yes," retorted Yasuo good-naturedly, continuing to shovel. "But you know, Aki-chan, you can't always bring your baby-sitter with you, can you?"

The woman was making tea on a portable stove. The boss and Kan continued marking off the site. Bent over like a farmer, Fujino was moving earth with the bamboo scoop. Yasuo leapt up out of the newly dug hole. Tattoos were visible on his arms where he had rolled up his sleeves.

The stink of Yasuo's underarms stung Akiyuki's nostrils. It choked him, made him nauseous. But he would keep on digging till he ran out of steam. He brought the pick down. It plunged cleanly through the earth. He guided it back up, and the earth rose, turning over. He put down the pick and took up the shovel. Putting his whole back into it, Akiyuki placed his foot on a corner of the shovel and dug down in. Then he lifted out the earth. He sweat. His sweat was still salty, and always, when he was digging, and his sweat stayed salty, it took an effort even to breathe. But once his sweat ran down like water, he felt completely at ease. His body got used to the digging, his breath adjusting to the rhythm of the work. Digging was what he liked most. More than anything, it made him feel he had truly worked. He liked its simplicity. The old-growth trees on the nearby mountain were stirring. Akiyuki swung the pick again, then shoveled up the earth, the muscles of his arms at work, the muscles of his stomach at work. Akiyuki felt like a man.

Listening to the banter of Yasuo and the woman, Akiyuki dug as deep as he could go. Damn, he liked to work hard with his body like this. It was the purest form of work. You start when the sun rises and quit when the sun sets. It was simple, even dirty, and sometimes you see stuff you'd never expect. Once they were cleaning out a big ditch next to a pig pen so they could build a stone wall. A puddle of pig piss lay at the bottom of the ditch. They got wet, soaked with it. The smell of the piss and all the other squishy filth almost overwhelmed the boss and the men, but not him. Then it happened. A sausage in a condom floated past them down through the ditch. Everybody perked up. Somewhere in the apartments behind the pig pen, or in the development, or even in a house in town, Akiyuki guessed, a young widow was moaning in constant frustration. "If only she'd call on us," remarked Yasuo.

Akiyuki dug. The earth swelled up. It split apart. Again he lifted the pick, and wielded it with all his strength. Drops of sweat ran into his eyes. Suddenly he looked up. For a second, he couldn't see a thing. Then, taking the towel tied around his head, he wiped away the sweat. His whole body was humming. He jumped up out of the pit.

"Sei-chan, give me some tea, too," he said to the woman, who was listening to Kan, on his break, talk about fishing. She laughed, showing the gap in her smile where her husband had supposedly knocked out a tooth, and poured tea from the kettle into a cup.

"Kan really knows his fishing," said the woman, handing Akiyuki the cup.

"Well, it's still a little early yet. Soon I'll be able to get trout in the mountains."

"The other day when I came to hang out with the boss at the Takada site, Akiyuki got a sweetfish," said Yasuo. "He got it in the rapids with a rock. Smashed in its head. There was another one dead without a mark on it. What'd ya do with that one?"

"Oh, I ate it. I took it to my sister's house and she said it gave her the creeps but she broiled it with salt for me."

"A big one?" asked the woman.

"What else? Akiyuki caught it," said Yasuo, winking in his direction.

"It was small. They were all babies," Akiyuki said.

Yasuo shook his head gravely. "I wonder," he pretended to whisper to himself. Then, still bent over, he extended his hands between his thighs and mumbled, "I bet it was about this long."

"Ah, whenever Yasu opens his mouth, I forget what we're supposed to be talking about," laughed the woman. Then everyone began to laugh. Akiyuki smiled uncomfortably. A curious fact dawned on him. Wherever he went, all anybody talked about was sex. The boss was watching him with a gleam in his eyes. Akiyuki looked away.

The trees were swaying, giving their leaves a gentle shake. Rid yourself of all excess—that's what he thought every time he had a wet dream. All he could hear now was the voices of the crew. Turning around, he could see the whole town spread below him. The station was right in the center, and from there roads stretched out crosswise with clusters of houses between. He could see the business district, too. There was a small hill to the left of the station, and below that was the alleyway where his sister's house stood. From there to his house you took the road along the railroad tracks and a path through the rice fields. A ten-minute walk. Then from his house the road continued straight to the windbreak forest, with other roads branching off on either side. Right near the forest was the cemetery, and Furuichi's house stood next to that, its white roof glinting in the sun. Beyond the windbreak was the beach. And then the sea. The town was shaped like a bucket turned open toward the water. The sun shone down, and it all seemed so strange to him. Everything, bathed in the same light. Everything, breathing in the same rhythm. Here, in such close quarters, they laughed, celebrated, groaned, violating and heaping abuse on one another. Even the ones most hated had a place here. The man was a good example. How many women had he reduced to tears, how many men wished him dead? The man—everybody talked about him—and Fumiaki's birth mother, too—both lived in this cramped little place. It amazed him. He felt stifled. Oppressed. The land was hemmed in by mountains and rivers and the sea, and the people lived on it like insects or dogs.

Akiyuki squatted down. The boss, sitting on a pile of lumber, moved over to make room and gestured for him to sit.

"Akiyuki, after lunch go and pick up the cement with Kan," he said.

"At Chōtoku?" Akiyuki asked.

"Yeah, that's right, Chōtoku," the boss said. "A girl there is crazy about you. Hey, Kan, isn't that right?"

But before everyone could laugh and tease him, Akiyuki said, "All the girls are crazy about me. I'm good-looking. And I'm nice to them."

"Yeah, yeah, lookin' good, he knows he's lookin' good!" said Yasuo.

❦

Just as they were pushing hard to make good progress before noon, Mitsuko could be seen bringing Yasuo's lunch. It was always the same. When the site was close to town, Mitsuko walked, and when it was further out, she rode a bicycle. Today she was wearing eyeliner and bright red lipstick, but sometimes she'd even have curlers in her hair. Walking around the pile of naked earth, she went and stopped by the propane stove. She gave a loud sigh.

"Yasuo, I'll leave it here," she called, putting down a new thermos lunchbox. "Oh, I'm tired."

She took a cigarette from a plastic case that belonged to one of the crew, and put it to her mouth. Then, crunching across some gravel in her sandals, she grabbed a match and lit the cigarette. She squatted down as Yasuo had been doing.

"Yasuo, you better come get me tonight like always. If you don't, I'm gonna cheat on you."

"You fool," said the boss. Mitsuko looked at the boss. Like peas in a pod, Akiyuki thought.

"Yasuo, now you work hard and bring home a bundle. If you work construction, you won't have to go to sea. We can always be together like we are now, but you have to really work hard. I'll bring you lunch," said Mitsuko. She blew smoke out her nose and ground out the cigarette on the dirt as if all she had wanted was a single puff. "And I won't even cheat on you. Hey, brother of mine, don't we look just like hot newlyweds close up?"

"You're so full of shit," said Yasuo. Again, the smell of Yasuo's armpits assailed Akiyuki.

"No, I'm serious," Mitsuko yawned. "Last night I went to bed at three and got up at six. I dozed off after Yasu left but I couldn't sleep because the kids next door were making such a ruckus."

She yawned again. This time she covered her mouth with her hand.

"Tonight I have to work at the bar again."

"Why not quit?" Kan and the boss, who had been measuring the pit, looked up. "Yasu has a job."

"I don't know when Yasu's going to tell me he's sick of con-struction and is going back to sea," said Mitsuko, her face now downcast. "I have to pay the rent. Hey, big brother number two, you tell Furuichi for me that just 'cause Daddy died he doesn't get to take over the house and the land. It's not like I'm asking for his right leg, the good one that didn't get all messed up in the truck accident. But Daddy was my Daddy, too. I'm his daughter. I have my rights."

"What's your fucking problem!" yelled the boss. "If that's all you're ever going to talk about, Mitsuko, I'm gonna beat the shit out of you."

"That's not all I ever talk about," Mitsuko apologized, flus-tered by the look on her brother's face. "I don't want to work at the bar. I just want to be with Yasu all the time like...we're newlyweds. I'm not just only going on about what I want. I'm saying, don't dump on other people. See, love is about the only thing I've got."

Mitsuko's thighs stuck out from her skirt as she squatted down. With the boss's scolding, her argument seemed to fall apart. The rhythm of the work on the site deteriorated too. Not only for Akiyuki but for the boss and the whole crew of six. Mitsuko squat-ted, looking distracted. Silently, Yasuo kept on shoveling.

⅋

The sun was just setting. Akiyuki put the tools away in the shed and washed his face and hands at the tap outside. After pouring water over his head he hunched down his dripping neck and went over to the back door of the house. "Sister, a towel, hand me a towel." Mie handed out a bath towel.

Mie's son, a sixth grader, came downstairs. "Let's go to Takada again soon, we'll catch more sweetfish."

"Yeah," Akiyuki said gruffly. He sat down on the raised step in the entryway and took off his work tabi.

"Akiyuki, what're you going to do? You want some sushi here?"

Mie was making a big dish of sushi. To sushi rice she added a generous amount of cooked fish, shiitake mushrooms, lotus root, and snow peas. She covered up the dish with plastic wrap and then wrapped it in a purple cloth. They often had this sushi for festivals, celebrations, and anniversaries. His mother made it, too.

"O.K., take it over there," laughed Mie as she handed him the big cloth-wrapped dish. Her smile was contagious. Mie lived in this house. Here in the place where the brother had died. Akiyuki remembered the time he had seen her naked. It wasn't long after her child was born. Mie had left the boss for cheating on her and had come home to her mother. That day, Mie had gone to take a bath. Innocently, Akiyuki had opened the door. She was washing her son. The right half of her back was deeply pitted with the scars of the pleurisy operation she'd had as a child. Akiyuki guessed the reason for the separation wasn't the boss's fooling around, it was his sister's back. But soon after that the couple got back together.

Mie's boy followed Akiyuki around the house asking what you needed to catch sweetfish in the rapids. The boss was shouting from the bathroom. Taking a change of clothes, Mie walked off in his direction.

"What are you going to do, Akiyuki?" she asked, looking back. And then, as if it had suddenly struck her, "Well, Mother and Father will be there, so I guess you should all eat together over there....Oh, not again," she said, looking past Akiyuki at the door.

Akiyuki looked around. Uncle Gen was standing there. Uncle Gen was the younger brother of the mother's first husband.

"Mie," Gen called.

"Coming, coming," Mie answered, "Just a minute, my husband's in the bath."

"I don't got any business with him," said Gen, glaring at her. He was drunk again.

Mie opened the bathroom door, dropped off the underwear, and returned quickly. She went to the refrigerator and took out a beer. "Here, Uncle, have one."

The boy snickered at the sight of Uncle Gen, who stood in the entranceway striking the heroic pose of some temple guardian figure. But Gen stood his ground, arms folded, glaring at Mie.

Akiyuki took the beer from his sister's hand and set it on the step up into the house. "Look, here," he said, but Gen didn't even glance at the bottle.

"Mie, look right into my eyes," Uncle Gen ordered. "You're not up to no good, are you? Nothing to make people hate you?"

"No, no, not even close. Come now, look at the beer I brought you."

"Drink it up, Uncle," Akiyuki said.

"It's not open," said Gen.

The boy laughed out loud.

"Hush," Mie scolded.

"Every so often I want to see Mie's face while I'm drinking. So today, I'll sit here and I'll have my drink."

Akiyuki stood up while Uncle Gen spoke. Mie looked nervous. What would Akiyuki do next? Akiyuki felt for his sister.

"A glass, a glass," Akiyuki said. "An opener and a glass," he repeated, walking into the kitchen. From the kitchen window he could see the last rays of the sunset. The sound of Uncle Gen's voice carried in.

"He's huge, he looks like a strongman. The spitting image of that man."

"Uncle, Akiyuki's my baby brother."

"Then I'll rest easy. 'Cause Mie has a strongman for a baby brother."

Uncle Gen sat down on the step. Akiyuki handed him the open beer bottle dripping with foam. Uncle Gen took the glass with his right hand and poured the beer with his left. He had no fingers on his right hand. The five fingers had fused together and then grown into two separate clumps of flesh. He'd been born that way. His hand made you think of an animal's hoof.

"Mie, if anything happens, just come and tell me. He might be your husband, but I'm unforgiving. One more girlfriend and it's instant death for him. I'm the king around here."

Holding the glass in his right hand seemed to pain him, so he switched to the left.

"The king of drunks," said the boy.

"Sssh," Mie scolded.

"What happened in your fight with city hall?" Akiyuki asked, taking his eyes off Uncle Gen's hand.

"I won that one too. I called the mayor, and after I gave him what for, he shut right up." Gen waved the hand.

"Yeah, so why'd they knock it down?" Akiyuki laughed.

Uncle Gen had built a shack on public land, and when the news got around a complaint came in from the city. Uncle Gen took up the fight. The last time Akiyuki ran into him, he vowed he wouldn't let any lousy bureaucrat ever lay a finger to it. But by the next day, the shack had been demolished. People said that Gen himself had agreed to it after a powerful person in the city had slipped him some cash. Uncle Gen downed the beer in one gulp.

"I'm the judge, I'm the law!"

The boss, who had gotten out of the bath and put on his long underwear, rubbed his head with a towel. "Then your law is all screwed up," he laughed.

"Screwed up, you think? You do anything bad and make Mie cry, it'll be instant death for you," Gen nodded to himself.

"Uncle, if you execute my man, I'm the one who'll suffer. I don't care what you do to others but at least go easy on him—if he's really really sorry and promises not to do it ever ever again."

"No can do, it's death for him. People who do bad things must die," pledged Uncle Gen, nodding in complete agreement with himself. "Yes, yes," he said watching Mie's reaction.

Neither Akiyuki nor Mie could figure out where Uncle Gen was getting his drink. He was the last living sibling of Mie's father. It was known that until four or five years ago, cloven-handed Uncle Gen and his wife had been running a candy store on a corner of the alleyway. All that time, Akiyuki never noticed the hand. He'd heard from his mother that one of the sisters' uncles had a deformed hand through some strange twist of fate, but he'd never seen it. Maybe Gen had been hiding it. Or maybe he had simply avoided going outside. It was only three years ago, after his wife died, that he'd started getting drunk and sponging alcohol from Mie.

Once Uncle Gen had come to Akiyuki's house and begged his mother for sake. She gave him a bottle, one of two they had put away for the stepfather's work crew. Uncle Gen guzzled one down and then asked for the other. Drinking that way will mess you up, Akiyuki's mother had said.

"I'm already a mess. Maybe that's the problem—you don't like your brother-in-law with his screwed up hand."

The mother grew angry. "What's it to me that you have a bad hand? My first husband is dead. How can I be related to a dead person?" The mother picked up a piece of kindling. "Don't think you can make a fool of me because I'm a woman. Do I have to hit you over the head with this?" She brandished the stick. Fumiaki, who happened to be home, stopped her. Later, when Mie learned what had happened, she bellowed out about her mother's cruelty and then set off for the mother's house, huffing that she would put her in her place. But by the time Akiyuki got there, Mie was in the room with the family altar, her face toward the wall, her shoulders hunched over, sobbing.

"Mie," said Uncle Gen, "Don't be a bad girl."

"Yes, yes, yes" Mie nodded, "I'm never bad." She poured beer into the glass.

Uncle Gen stared at Mie's son and opened his eyes wide like a clown.

"Boy, shall I tell you a story?"

The boy nodded.

"There's a tengu, a demon, in those mountains over there. I'm always talking to him. His face is all red. So when I go there drunk, he thinks I'm one of his buddies and he tells me all kinds of things. He knows everything. Those two guys got in a fight today. That guy did something bad. That guy's going to die."

"What a bunch of shit," Akiyuki laughed.

Akiyuki felt uneasy. Here was Gen, taking advantage of Mie's kindness and making her suffer. When Uncle Gen had finished his beer, the boss asked Mie to bring him another. Mie took one out of the refrigerator. Akiyuki stood up. There on the small Buddhist altar was a photo of his half-siblings' father. Age the photo, smudge it, add wrinkles, and you'd have Uncle Gen, he thought.

Akiyuki took the sushi and left the boss's house. The sun had set.

Purposely taking the long way, he passed through the red-light district. He felt a sweet fatigue. Women were standing in the alley soliciting customers. The rumor popped into his mind: a young woman who was either the latest girlfriend of that man, his natural father, or his own half-sister born to a whore was said to be working at a bar in the neighborhood. Sometime, he thought, I'll go to that bar. But for now he had no thought of meeting her. What would be the point? He couldn't even imagine it.

The alley in the red-light district smelled faintly of sewage and piss. "Come here, handsome," a woman called to him. He didn't answer. "Stop in for a while," said the woman, now taking him by the arm. He could smell makeup and liquor. He had money. Enough money to get drunk and buy a woman. But he'd never had a woman and he didn't want one now. Didn't want to dirty himself in something pointless and messy. No, no, he worried that if he did it just once, he'd become obsessed with it and end up with his mind in the sewer just like that man, who couldn't keep his hands to himself.

"Come in, I'll give you a deal," said the woman pulling at his hand. The tree at the corner of the alley was shaking. Akiyuki's breath was ragged. C'mon, pull my arm one more time, he thought, then I'll get drunk and hold a woman for the first time, for real and not in my dreams. Really know a woman for the first time. Overflow. But the woman let go of his arm.

"I'm broke," Akiyuki said.

The woman looked away.

Two doors down was a bar that his brother had been known to frequent when he was alive. The Yayoi. Akiyuki hurried past it. He sensed he was being watched, and he felt forbidden to enter the bar, or even to walk in front of it. Then the sound of his own footsteps reassured him, and he turned toward home. A white flower was blooming in the darkness. It looked like somebody's face. Akiyuki's older brother had died at the age he was now. But he couldn't believe that he looked like him, as his mother and sister always said he did. Akiyuki was big. With rough hands and feet. His eyes looked like knots in a slab of wood, and his nose was the snout of a lion. This body, this face—no way could he look like his brother. His brother had had a beautiful face, a mix of the father, Uncle Gen, and the mother. But Akiyuki's face belonged to that man. The ugliest face in the world, the crudest face, a face full of evil, Akiyuki thought to himself. That man, always watching him from a distance. Always chasing him. Akiyuki stopped in his tracks. A desire to meet the child of the whore swept over him. I'll go to the Yayoi and see for myself, he thought. But even if the woman learned she was his half-sister, nothing would come of it. He'd been brought up among half-siblings, and now he was living with the mother's second husband, his stepfather he called "Father," and the stepfather's son he called "Brother." The child of the whore would become a whore. The child in the construction worker's house would became a construction worker. That was the simplest way. Akiyuki picked up his pace. But even as he was surrounded by all sorts of brothers and sisters, mothers and fathers, he couldn't believe he was the only one in the world who felt the way he did.

🗝

Construction work suits Akiyuki. All day long he digs and shovels up earth. Sometimes he makes concrete by putting sand, gravel, and cement in a mixer, and where they can't take the mixer, he makes the concrete on an iron plate with a shovel. Sometimes he and the crew fix bumpy roads. Akiyuki works all day long. Seated on the ground, he has a smoke. Eats a meal. The sun is hot. A breeze feels pleasant on his sweaty skin. He doesn't think. The tips of the branches quiver. Now, it's back to work. Break up the earth. How much depends on how hard you swing the pick! Then you shovel. Again, it all depends on how you place your hips and how strong your arms are. It's straightforward. The earth isn't wrinkled like the human heart. Akiyuki liked construction work.

That day it started to rain in the afternoon. The rain was depressing, so after Akiyuki stopped working he went straight home. The stepfather and Fumiaki were out. He heated water, took a bath, and then ate a very early supper by himself. His mother mentioned that Mie had been there until just before it began to rain. "The memorial service will cheer her up," she said. For a long time the mother had been planning the service for her first husband, the father of the sisters, and now only a month remained. Akiyuki sat eating in his underwear. "Yoshiko called from Nagoya. She said that since it's a memorial service for *their* father we should do it at Mie's house, but I couldn't bear doing it there." She abruptly lowered her voice. "When I got the call from Yoshiko, I just wanted to cry. I'll do the service here but I'll leave everything up to Mie. They'll even bring their own priest. We won't use ours. "

The mother stood up and turned off the gas in the kitchen.

"What does it matter?" Akiyuki said.

"Maybe it doesn't matter, but it's tricky enough us just getting along with each other."

The mother sat down. She made him think of a pregnant dog. Outside the rain was coming down lightly. Inside the house was thick with gloom. The stepfather's trousers were hanging from the doorframe. Somewhere in the distance, an engine was idling.

After supper Akiyuki had absolutely nothing to do. He lay down in the room with the altar and the television. The mother brought out a pillow and a light quilt. She sat down by the pillow.

"Just be patient for five more years," the mother said. "In the meantime you can settle down, have some kids, and then go out on your own. But until then, you're an apprentice. You can't drink and gamble with the crew. That's my biggest worry—you drinking and gambling."

"I don't drink, and I don't gamble. That's not what I like to do."

"Is that possible?" she laughed. "But I can see it in your face. You'd like to try."

"Sounds like you're egging me on."

"Don't be stupid. What parent would do that to their own child? Do you know anybody who has suffered more from drinking and gambling personally than me?" She laughed, but sent him an angry glance. "If you just think of yourself as a worker, you won't ever make it to contractor. Look at your stepfather," the mother said. "He only has a couple drinks after work and he doesn't gamble. Make yourself into a good contractor. Your older brother, too," she said, referring to Fumiaki. "You can join forces and take over your stepfather's business, or if you don't want to, you can go out on your own. I'll support you. That's my job."

"If I lived with that man, I'd be a big landowner's bratty kid now, wouldn't I?"

The words slipped out of Akiyuki's mouth. The mother's expression changed instantly.

"What a bastard! Things won't go well for him. How could they?" The mother spoke now as if the man were standing right behind Akiyuki. "Cheating people out of things, pretending they were his all along! Every time I hear another rumor about him I want to rip you open and drain out half your blood!"

She was excited now. Akiyuki stared at her.

Just then the front door banged opened. The mother turned around. It was the stepfather. His work clothes were all soaked through. He looked wide-eyed at the mother.

"A terrible thing has happened.... Toki, a terrible thing," he repeated, swallowing the words. "Furuichi's been stabbed."

The stepfather went straight to the top of the cabinet and grabbed the keys to the motorcycle.

Akiyuki got up.

"Who did it?" he asked.

"Yasuo," said the stepfather. "I'm going right to the hospital."

"What about Mie?" the mother asked.

"I don't know," said the stepfather. "I'm going to the hospital."

"What about Mie? Father, what about Mie?" said the mother.

"I don't know, I don't know," he said.

It was raining. Akiyuki, wearing nothing but pants and a T-shirt, dashed outside and ran to his sister's house. Vaguely he sensed he was cold. Soon he was out of breath. But he kept running. Small drops of rain pelted his face. He couldn't understand it. How could such a thing have happened so suddenly? Mitsuko's husband, Yasuo, had stabbed his wife's and the boss's older brother. Why had perfectly healthy Yasuo attacked Furuichi, a cripple with a wooden leg? Had his stepfather seen it happen? Had he heard about it from someone?

The greenery on the little hill shone wet with rain.

First, Akiyuki had to find out whether it was true or not. He knew the relationship between Mitsuko and Furuichi was much worse than that between Mitsuko and the boss or the boss and Furuichi. But why did Yasuo have to stab him?

The only one home at Mie's house was her son. He was sprawled on the tatami reading a comic book. Akiyuki was disappointed. Soaking wet, he stepped up into the house. People would have been gathering there, the police would be on the scene, and his sister would be in shock, crying, her hair in a mess. This is what he had imagined.

"Where's my sister?" he asked the boy. Without looking up the boy replied, "The hospital."

"Was he really stabbed?"

"Yeah," the boy looked up for the first time, "Blood all over him. They picked him up."

"Who?" he yelled.

"Uncle Yasuo. Uncle Furuichi went to the hospital. Everybody's there now."

Akiyuki hesitated. He was soaked to the skin. It was still pouring outside. But the sky was strangely light. He smoked a cigarette. Yasuo had stabbed Furuichi. Blood gushing everywhere. He could imagine it well enough without having to see it. If you're stabbed, you bleed. If you bleed too much, you die. He didn't care much about Furuichi. It was Mie who worried him. She'd always been weak physically. Her whole life she'd been prone to fevers and vomiting. She also had a morbid obsession about cleanliness; he had wondered how she could function as the wife of a construction worker. A single hair in a bowl of rice made her blanche, and the sight of plucked chicken skin unnerved her. How would she react to the sight of a human being losing huge amounts of blood? He should be there with her. He rubbed his head with a bath towel. As he took the towel from his face, he saw Uncle Gen standing there in the rain holding an umbrella.

"Mie, Mie," he yelled.

"Uncle, she's not here," Akiyuki said sticking his head out the window. "You can't drink here today."

"Mie, Mie," Uncle Gen called. He was weaving back and forth, barely able to stand. He was wearing sandals, but his feet were slashed to ribbons and black with mud.

"She's not here, she's not here," Akiyuki said.

Uncle Gen ignored him. "Mie, are you doing something bad? Are people going to hate you?"

Hearing Gen's voice, the boy snorted.

⚜

Mie was at the hospital.

"At last you're here," she said when she saw Akiyuki. She led him to the nurse's room. Furuichi's wife and young daughter were there. The wife was holding the girl and crying. The girl opened her eyes wide like a dog's at the sight of Akiyuki.

"Take Furuichi's wife to my house and let her rest."

"I don't want to!" said the wife shaking her head. "My husband's dying. I don't want to!" she screamed.

The daughter was staring at Akiyuki as if he were her father's murderer. Her eyes were dry.

"It's O.K. He's not going to die. They're giving him a transfusion now."

"I don't want to—he's going to die," the wife said, shaking her head.

"He's O.K. He's not going to die," said Mie decisively.

"He's going to die, he's going to die," the wife repeated.

Akiyuki was standing behind his sister.

"Everybody gave blood for the transfusion. There's no way he can die," Mie said comforting the wife. She sounded convinced.

Akiyuki followed his sister out of the room. Furuichi was in the operating room, she said. They stopped close by.

"What are you going to do?" Mie asked.

He shook his head.

"Give Mother a message for me, will you? Furuichi's wife is in such a state, I better be here for a while, but could she take care of the daughter?"

"I'll tell her," he answered.

"Give her dinner and a bath over there, and then she can sleep at my house."

"What about breakfast tomorrow before school?"

"Hmm, let me see," Mie considered. "O.K., I'll make some time to go and take care of her. Just for today give her supper over there."

Akiyuki couldn't figure out what had caused it. It had just happened out of the blue. He could see Yasuo before him. No, what he remembered was the musty smell emanating from Yasuo's armpits when he worked. That day they had worked together until the rain started. It was the same as always. They were preparing to pour concrete that afternoon. Then they got slowed down. Mitsuko climbed up the mountain path to the site carrying Yasuo's lunch box. Once she arrived, the crew started clowning around. They ate lunch after she left. Thick clouds had gathered, blocking the sun. But the wind blew as always, rustling the tips of the branches and the leaves. They had finished getting ready and were just about to pour when the rain started. That was it. The job had to be put off until the next day. So they stopped work. But what had happened to Yasuo after that? Yasuo stabs Furuichi. Furuichi bleeds. Yasuo stabs him again. Furuichi's wife and daughter begin to wail.

Akiyuki was sitting on a bench in the waiting room. An old woman with her thin hair pulled back in a bun was talking to the receptionist. His clothes were nearly dry, he realized. His stepfather walked toward him from the interior of the hospital. Akiyuki stood up. The stepfather caught sight of him.

"It looks very bad. He's not going to make it. They're giving him a transfusion. Still, even if they save him, they'll have to cut off his other leg."

"Where was he stabbed?" Akiyuki asked gruffly.

"In his leg, his thigh. A number of times. Even if they save him, he'll be a complete cripple. What a cruel thing to do."

Mie came hurrying down the hall.

"Father, tell Mother not to worry," she said.

The stepfather nodded.

⚜

Afterward they learned that Yasuo had stabbed Furuichi three times in his good leg. Everybody said that Mitsuko had put him up to it. Only three hours had passed since Akiyuki had put away the tools in the boss's shed and said good-bye to Yasuo. But in that time, the world had turned upside down.

Furuichi died. The funeral was held at his home on the beach. Akiyuki watched Mie. Her shoulders sagged. She sat there listless.

It was humid. The priest was chanting sutras. The windows were open but the funeral wreaths standing in front of them cut off the breeze. Akiyuki went outside. Across the street from the beach house was a pile of logs. A buzz saw sounded. Akiyuki lit a cigarette. For a while he sat on the logs listening to the buzz saw and the chanting of the sutras. The sun was strong, nearly blinding. Suddenly it came to him. His brother had wanted to do to him and his mother what Yasuo had done to Furuichi. Time and time again, his brother had come to the house with a kitchen knife. Sometimes he came with an ax. Akiyuki could remember it as if it had all happened yesterday. He was twelve. His brother was twenty-four, his age now. It was early morning and the wooden shutters were still closed. No lights were on. He woke to the sound of his mother's voice. She was sitting erect on the futon in her nightclothes. The stepfather sat cross-legged next to her. Akiyuki and Fumiaki were sleeping in the next room. He knew that his brother had come. The brother was drunk again.

"You hate it that Akiyuki and I are doing well?"

"Yeah, I hate it," said the brother. "You two did what's best for you."

"The two of us, you say, but Akiyuki's still a child. Aren't you and Mie and Yoshiko already grown up?"

"So it's O.K to throw us away? You do what's best for you, bring Akiyuki with you, and then just abandon the rest of us?"

"But Akiyuki's still a child and you're grown up, aren't you?"

"That's how you played it all along. You dumped us, took Akiyuki with you, and ran off with this guy. I remember everything. Yoshiko and Mie were Akiyuki's age now. I don't forget a thing!" The brother yelled. His voice was shaking. "I'm going to kill you!"

Akiyuki didn't feel sad but he tried to make himself cry anyway. Maybe that way, he thought, his brother would calm down. Fumiaki, who was sleeping in the next futon, reached out and covered Akiyuki's mouth with his hand.

"Akiyuki, you come here too, you fucking traitor," the brother called.

Still lying down, Fumiaki pinned Akiyuki down with one arm, urging him not to go. Akiyuki pushed off Fumiaki's arm and opened the sliding door. The brother had a knife in his hand.

"Sit there," said the brother, plunging the knife into the tatami. Akiyuki stopped crying.

"So you two get to be happy, but the rest of us don't matter?"

"You're adults," said the mother.

"Oh, so it's O.K. to throw children away like puppy dogs? It's O.K. to leave the girls without even seeing them married?"

"You're adults, aren't you? I couldn't afford big dowries anyway, but they've done well for themselves, haven't they," insisted the mother. "If you're so full of hatred, then kill me and Akiyuki. If you want to, go ahead, just do it."

"Oh, I will, I'm going to kill you."

The brother pulled the knife out of the tatami and held it tight.

"Stop, stop," croaked the stepfather, his voice faltering.

"Shut up!" The brother drove the knife back into the tatami. "I don't want to hear any shit from you. Keep your mouth shut."

"If you want to kill me, go ahead," said the mother. "I can't stand to see you like this. My own child telling me he hates me. The child of my womb spitting out how he wants to kill me—I can't bear it. It's up to you. If you want to stab me with that knife, go ahead and do it.... I'm ashamed to have your stepfather and Fumiaki see this."

That time it didn't go any further. Another time, Mie was there with the brother, and she was able to get him to cool down. But then, directing her words more to Mie than the brother, the mother said, "If you're all going to act this way, you're no children of mine." Mie crumpled, weeping.

That time too, it had seemed strange to Akiyuki that Mie would weep as if it had all been her fault.

That year on Girl's Day, without warning, the brother hanged himself from a tree in the garden. It was a cold day. Mie came to the house. Saying nothing, she suddenly hugged the mother. Mie's breath hung white in the air. She didn't speak about her sorrow. Akiyuki watched them both. It had ended too soon. So many times the brother had come to the house with a knife or an ax to kill the mother and himself, and now the brother's life had been cut short before he had seen the blood and heard the screams of those he detested. Twelve years had passed. Akiyuki was twenty-four. The boy born to Mie the year the brother died was now twelve. Some things had changed completely. And some things were just the way they'd been twelve years ago.

He stared at the house by the beach. The sun washed over him. It didn't make sense that someone had been stabbed here. What could explain a man being stabbed three times in his one remaining good leg?

There were about fifteen big wreaths outside the house. Akiyuki watched the neighborhood children peeking in from the entranceway. Their eyes were bright.

"Akiyuki," a voice called.

It was Fumiaki.

"Get Father for me."

"What, you need him for something?"

"It's work," said Fumiaki.

Akiyuki stood up. He went inside and over to his stepfather, who was seated by the family altar. "Excuse me, but..."

The coffin itself looked like Furuichi's body. The altar held a photo of a smiling Furuichi. The mother sat next to the stepfather. On her other side was Mie. Mie looked just like her mother. If the mother shed pounds and years, they would be identical. The stepfather went outside. They were short on some equipment and Fumiaki asked whom he should call to get some more.

"You don't even know that?" said the stepfather. "Call Yamaki. You put so much energy into having a good time that you don't have any left for work."

"Well how am I supposed to know that? You do everything by yourself and then out of the blue you give an order," Fumiaki muttered.

"Hey, you, watch your mouth," said the stepfather as Fumiaki walked off toward a small van. His prayer beads in one hand, the stepfather bent down and picked up a stone. "How dare you talk to your father that way," he said, throwing the stone as if to chase him away. The stone flew close to Fumiaki's backside but just missed.

At that moment, the hearse came slowly over the bridge. The stepfather stood in front of the house.

"Out of the way!" he yelled, waving his hands.

Fumiaki revved up the van's engine, backed up forcefully, honked the horn once, turned around, and sped off toward the coast. Then the hearse backed in.

෫

Akiyuki must have been dreaming. In the middle of the dream he willed himself to remember it. But by the time he woke up he had forgotten. Fumiaki looked at him, laughing. The sun was streaming in. He felt something had changed, but nothing about the morning was any different.

"Hurry up, Akiyuki," said the mother.

It seemed odd to him that the dead would never know this morning. He could smell the dried fish on the grill. If, that day, he had been murdered by his brother, he wouldn't be able to see this morning, wouldn't be able to feel it.

Mie's house was shuttered up tight. He'd never seen it like this before and didn't know what to do. Should he knock on the door and wake them up? Maybe they were taking the day off after the funeral. Even if they weren't, the work had gotten all screwed up since the rainy day, the day that Yasuo stabbed Furuichi. If they didn't pour concrete that day, they couldn't go on to their next job. Akiyuki thought to himself as he sat down in front of the closed glass front door. A dog came out of a side alley. They could work without the boss. With himself, Kan, Fujino, and the woman, they'd be fine. All they needed were the keys to the shed and the van. He spotted Fujino walking toward him from the railroad crossing. Akiyuki relaxed. Through work, they'd go back to the old life—start in the morning when the sun rises and finish in the evening when the sun sets. That's what he hoped. People just can't go around stabbing each other. The best thing would be to forget about it right now and not dredge it up anymore.

Noticing that the shutters of the boss's house were still closed, Fujino said, "The boss and his wife must be tired."

"We have to pour concrete today," Akiyuki said.

"They'll get up soon. Give 'em a little time."

The woman and Kan had come.

"So, we're back to work today," said Kan. "Pretty drastic thing Yasuo did."

"He didn't intend to kill him," said the woman. "It seems he went after him with the knife just to scare him."

The glass door rattled. It was being unlocked from the inside and then it opened. The boss looked out, naked from the waist up.

"Ah, you're all here," he said rubbing his eyes. "Mie, I'm going to tell your mother to come over here later. Also, I'm going to phone the doctor and tell him to come. You stay in bed today."

Then, looking at the faces of the crew, the boss apologized, "Last night she ran a fever. She's not very strong." His face drooped.

"Is she sick?" Akiyuki asked.

"I have a cold." Mie's voice sounded from inside. Her voice was raspy from the phlegm in her throat.

"She's probably just worn out," said the boss, "Akiyuki, open the shed for me." He handed over the keys. The metal felt cold on Akiyuki's hand.

The crew was strangely subdued at the ten o'clock break, at lunchtime, and at the three o'clock break, too. If somebody made a joke, the others lowered their voices as if they were trading secrets. It was because Yasuo wasn't there. He had had enough spirit for four people. His arms might have been covered in tattoos, but he had never seemed like the murdering type.

When the boss wasn't around, one of the crew murmured, "Mitsuko put him up to it." Yasuo had been trapped. The real victim was Yasuo. The workers sympathized more with Yasuo than with the man who had died of his stab wounds.

"Well, Yasuo won't be able to see Mitsuko for a long time. Much longer than when he went to sea," said Kan.

The sight of the crew enjoying this gossip made no sense to Akiyuki. If he stabbed somebody, would they gossip about him afterward? He turned the mixer on. He loaded six buckets of gravel, three buckets of sand, and one small bucket of cement into the mixer's cage, and then he added water. Six to three to one— that was the ratio. The mixer ground the ingredients smoothly. Akiyuki was in charge of the mixer. Fujino collected the newly made concrete in a wheelbarrow and carried it off. The boss and Kan spread the concrete. The woman was in charge of getting water and raking through the sand.

"It's soft," said Fujino.

Akiyuki gave an order to the woman, who dumped three heaping buckets of sand and water into the mixer. Taking over for her, Akiyuki threw in a bucket of cement and more gravel, too. Then, as if in a rush to get the next load done, he raked new gravel into the empty cage and measured out cement into a bucket. When Yasuo was there and there were plenty of workers to do the various jobs, all Akiyuki had to worry about was filling buckets with cement and water. Then, just at the right moment, he would put the sand prepared by the woman and the gravel prepared by Yasuo into the mixer. The time he had gotten into a fight with Fumiaki when he was still on his stepfather's crew had been over this job. It was the crucial position for making concrete. His mix was neither too hard nor too soft. The boss often praised it as being the best concrete around. But this day, things didn't go his way. It was already five o'clock when they finished the job, but they'd never gotten it to the right consistency.

"Hey, we'd better get someone to replace Yasuo or we won't

get any work done," said the woman. Her look implied that she wanted him to tell the boss they needed another worker. Akiyuki kept gathering the tools. Now that they had poured the concrete, he expected they wouldn't come back to this site for a while. The next day they were scheduled to contour a hill and build a wall at a girls' school. The boss and Kan would continue on here, taking a couple days to finish up. They could leave the mixer where it was and have Yamaki, who owned the tool shop, come and pick it up. Akiyuki knew old Yamaki. Whenever he went with Kan to buy tools or lease a bulldozer or a dump truck, he could feel Yamaki glaring at him with hate in his eyes as if to say, "So you're one of that man's children." Only recently the man had extorted a promissory note from Yamaki, and he had almost lost his business.

Akiyuki got a ride in the boss's van. He sat in the passenger's seat. The boss was silent. They took the shortest route home. Until today at least one time out of three they had gone the long way around for Yasuo and taken the road to his apartment.

"Boss, Mitsuko was in a bad mood this morning," Yasuo would say, asking to be let out somewhere along the way. But at those times the boss would deliberately bring the van to a stop at Yasuo's door.

As they rounded the corner, they came to the main business district. The van turned right at the light and continued down a straight road, the speedometer hovering at 40. Above them the clouds were turning crimson and gold. The green of the trees had been visible a minute ago, but now the mountains were fading to black. It gave Akiyuki the jitters. He needed someone to hold him steady. Something had changed. Something had broken. But what? He felt weariness wash over him. The boss, Kan, Fujino, and even the woman, who often laughed, rode on in silence.

☙

Since the day after the funeral, Mie had been sick with exhaustion and a cold. The excitement over the murder hadn't died down yet, so people sympathized with her. She, the bedridden sister, ill with fatigue, anxiety, and a cold, was the real victim, more so than the murderer and the dead Furuichi. The doctor said her pleurisy had come back, and when she heard this, Mie wept. It was the worst possible news. Akiyuki understood Mie's feelings only too well.

Mie had come down with pleurisy around the age of four. There wasn't much they could do, the doctor had said. Mie herself had told the story over and over again. Every day when her father came home from work, he had barely taken his jacket off before he began stroking her feverish, wasted body as she struggled for breath.

"There my sweetheart, there, there," the father said.

Unable to cry, Mie moaned faintly. The father sold some property in the mountains, and with that money paid for the doctors to take out three of her ribs and operate on her lungs. Mie survived. But within about a year the father was dead, leaving them absolutely nothing. This part Mie must have heard from the mother. But now all she spoke about was the father calling her "sweetheart." At such times her eyes filled with tears.

After Mie fell ill, the mother came by frequently. She cooked meals, did the laundry, and cleaned the house. Then she would sit by Mie's futon and await the time when Akiyuki would arrive to put away his tools.

Mie pulled the quilt up around her neck. She was very pale. "Welcome back," called the mother, noticing that Akiyuki had come into the house. "Mie and I were just talking about when you were born."

"He's grown to look a lot like Brother." Mie raised her head to see him. She turned on her side and tried to get up, but the mother stopped her.

"How's work?" asked Mie.

"We're done. But if the mason doesn't come tomorrow, we can't move on."

"Just like my husband says. When it comes to work, Akiyuki really gives a hundred percent," said Mie to the mother.

"And if he doesn't, he won't become a contractor," said the mother. As if to herself, she continued on. "Even now, I remember it like it was yesterday. When I broke up with that man, I was six months pregnant, and I was wondering how I was going to make it. Your brother, Yoshiko, and you were saying, have the baby, have the baby. To you all it was like having a doll— you weren't going to be bringing it up though. But I worried because the child would only be a half-brother or -sister to you and you might reject it, and what's more, I had to feed all of you. Anyway, I decided to have the baby. Then your brother got demanding. 'Have a boy, have a boy. I don't want a girl, they cry all the time.'"

"Brother got mad at me all the time for being a crybaby. But the only time you were nice to us was when we were sick."

"If I'd been nice to you like the other mothers we'd have starved to death. It was just after the war and I had to go out to the countryside and get stuff to sell. I had nothing to fall back on like other women. I got together with Tomi from Irie—the one who's so respectable now—and we went out getting some potatoes here, some persimmons there. She was pregnant at the time, too. It was perfect, we were even. We got to a temple and the priest said, 'Oh you're pregnant' and gave us rice cakes. He looked at both our bellies. Times are hard, he said, but try to have healthy babies. Then he stared hard into our faces. Here's a white one for you, he told me, because you look like you're going to have a boy, and he gave a red one to Tomi because she looked like she was going to have a girl. It made me so happy."

The mother stretched out her legs and changed position. She looked at him.

"Tomi was so disappointed. All she had was girls. 'Toki, do you think it's a girl?' she said. 'Don't worry,' I said 'That's just superstition,' I said. But to myself I was thinking, 'It's a boy, I'm going to have a boy.' I don't know how many pounds of potatoes I carried home on my back that day, but I didn't feel a thing. I showed your brother the rice cake and told him the story. He was thrilled...."

"That priest must be dead by now," said Mie sadly.

"He would have been around seventy at the time."

"I want to go back to the old days," said Mie. Her eyes filled with tears. "Everybody was alive back then."

"I feel the same way," said the mother looking into Akiyuki's face. "Has it really been twenty-four years?"

"After Akiyuki was born, you went out to work so soon, it's like I was Akiyuki's mother. Boy, he'd scream when he was hungry." Mie glanced at the mother. "Were you already seeing our stepfather back then?"

"How could I have?" said the mother pounding Akiyuki's stretched out legs lightly. Then she squeezed his shins.

"I'd had my fill of men back then. How could I depend on a man? That's why I went out selling things every day."

"Hmm, so that's how it was," said Mie. "You'd go out selling things, and when Akiyuki started crying with hunger and you didn't come back for a while, I'd send out Brother or Yoshiko to find you, and then I'd hold that screaming baby tight, and we'd cry huddled together on the floor. First I'd give him cold water, then hot water, but he'd start wailing pretty soon. We were hungry enough but the worst thing was Akiyuki's crying."

"I got together with your stepfather when Akiyuki was a toddler. While I was out making the rounds selling, I found out he was bringing up Fumiaki without a woman's hand...." She pounded Akiyuki lightly on the legs again.

"They were all alive back then—all the fun people," said Mie, and then she sat up as if she meant to change the subject. The white of her nightgown looked blue.

"For some reason, having Mother here all the time taking care of me, I feel like I'm back in the old days. Any minute Daddy will walk through that door," Mie laughed. "A little while ago when Mother went to the store, I was dozing. Uncle Gen was outside, drunk again, calling 'Mie, Mie,' in that big old voice of his. You know, he sounds like Daddy. In my dream, I was a baby again. Daddy, Mie's sick again. The pleurisy is back. I've gotten it again. Daddy, I can't talk very much. That's what I'd say and then I'd burst out crying—Daddy, Daddy."

She was crying as she spoke. She'd been dozing and dreaming, the sound of Uncle Gen's voice carrying her back to the old days when her father was still alive and she'd been sick, and then she started to cry.... Akiyuki could just picture this happening to her. Nobody's home. Her husband's at work and her child's in school. In the middle of the day her mother, who's taking care of her, goes off shopping. "Mie, Mie, have you done something that makes you ashamed to see me?" Uncle Gen calls. Akiyuki could imagine the sound of Uncle Gen's voice. "I won't let you get away with anything really bad, but I'll forgive you if you were a little bad because you're Mie," says Uncle Gen. He's so drunk that he's weaving and can barely stand. Crash!... he falls backward against the glass front door. Suddenly, Mie wakes from her dream. Uncle Gen is there, calling her name. She gets up. She has a fever.

"Did you give him something to drink?" asked the mother.

Mie nodded. "He's fallen pretty low, but he's still my uncle."

"You shouldn't," said the mother. "He'll be back."

"It doesn't cost me much. He's the only one I give it to, so I thought it would be O.K. I'm repaying my debt to my parents."

"I understand how you feel. But you don't have to repay a debt to someone who isn't even your parent."

"Well, I sure haven't repaid you," Mie laughed. "I'm not healthy and I'm a crybaby on top of it."

த

Akiyuki walked home with his mother, his tabi softly tapping on the pavement. He felt somebody was watching them. But who? The brother who had come so many times with a knife to murder them all but in the end had hanged himself? Or that man? If only he could take his mother to that bar and make sure. The woman in the red-light district. What did she look like? The mother had seen the child who was born to the whore and to the man who was his natural father. The child was his half-sister, and the mother would be able to pick her out immediately. She had told him about it some time ago. Or maybe he'd heard the story from his sister. The man was in jail. He'd been arrested for gambling. The mother found out that there were two other women, so when she was six months pregnant she went to the jail. "From now on, I'll have nothing to do with you. I'll have the child without you and raise it myself, three or four children—what's the difference anyway," she told the man. So while he was in jail, three children, linked only by his blood, were born one after another to differ-ent mothers. Among the three, he was the only boy, meaning he was not only the man's first child but his first son. The mother had broken things off, and the prostitute was leaving town, too, so when the man came out of jail, the mother formally handed him over to the proper young woman. The prostitute, saying she would purify her body and go home to the mountains, brought her little baby girl to see them before she left. The mother showed off her child, too.

"Look, it's your big brother," said the prostitute to the baby girl, who was swaddled in a red quilt. The baby was his half-sister. So supposedly he had seen her. But Akiyuki didn't remember. If he met her now, they wouldn't feel like brother and sister, but at least he wanted to make sure. He looked at his mother. It was a cruel thing she had done, he thought.

The mother walked quickly. Perhaps, he guessed, she was feeling sorry for the stepfather.

"Mie's a weakling and a crybaby," Akiyuki said.

The mother's steps slowed.

"Don't ask me why, but I'm feeling angry." Her eyes flashed. "How could I have let her marry into such a terrible family! You know how she is—she thinks too much about other people and then she suffers. As for Yasuo and Mitsuko, they can put them to death for all I care. Worthless, good-for-nothings."

🜍

For a while Mie's pleurisy seemed to have made her revert to her old weak, weepy self. But it turned out that the doctor had made a mistake. It was just a cold that had taken a turn for the worse. "Thank goodness, thank goodness," rejoiced Mie to herself.

They were in the room where they usually hung laundry and stored the beer and sake they would give away in the new year. The rain shutters were open. Mie's cheeks were rosy. Maybe because she wasn't wearing makeup, you could see her freckles, too.

"If I'd gotten pleurisy again, I would have died. It frightens me more than anything else," Mie said.

"He charges a fortune and feeds you a bunch of bullshit," said the boss.

With Mie's recovery, life slowly began to return to normal. Or so Akiyuki thought. But since the incident with Yasuo, the crew never joked around anymore. Each morning they gathered at Mie's house, got the keys from the boss, took out the tools, and loaded up the van. In the evening, they put the tools back in the shed. They didn't clown around or drink together, but instead went straight home. Only now Mitsuko and Yasuo weren't there.

The woman worker had come into the boss's house and was looking for the crews' teacups. The mother had completely taken over the kitchen, and now that she was gone the teacups couldn't be found.

"Excuse me, where are the teacups? They're not in the usual place and they're not on the shelf. The boss is saying we should have a cup of tea, but we can't if we don't find them," said the woman.

"Hmm. Where could they be? Keep looking," said Mie from her futon. Akiyuki came in and took a guess. He knew his mother through and through; she wouldn't store the workers' cups where things for the family were kept. He opened the door under the sink. The cups were on a tray on top of the pickle jar. They were wet.

"Here they are." He spoke loudly as if to atone for his mother's behavior.

With Mie still in bed, the crew couldn't drink sake in the house after work. So they installed a lamp in the shed and spread out a mat. The place reeked of iron and coal. They grilled dried fish on a portable stove and drank a bottle of cold sake. The sake was sweet on the tongue. They were a party of four. The woman downed a whole cup of sake but looked sober.

"Delicious," she said, "Things have really gone bad for us what with the boss's wife getting sick and all. When I saw the look on the boss's face, I'd have traded places with him if I could."

"She's the one who has suffered the most," said Kan.

"At first I couldn't believe it, I came running when I heard the news about Yasuo. It couldn't be true, I thought, but it was. Kan and I were all crazy and we ran to the doctor's. I got out of breath, but Kan, well, he's younger after all," said Fujino.

"I ran, too," Akiyuki said, "and it was pissing down rain."

"Hey, if it hadn't rained and we'd poured that concrete, Yasuo wouldn't have done what he did. We never know what's going to happen to us, do we?...Poor Furuichi—being stabbed like that right in front of his wife and kid."

The woman's words reminded Akiyuki again of the times his older brother had come to the house with a knife. The brother hadn't been able to kill them, hadn't even left a mark on them. Akiyuki drained his cup of sake. It made his stomach tingle hotly, and then it passed through his intestines, and down into his groin. He could smell the sweat in his undershirt.

"Rain sucks," he said. He looked up. The hair on Kan and Fujino's faces stood out in the lamplight.

"Fuckin' rain."

"Yeah, but what can you do? It rains a lot around here. And you can't work when it does."

The woman poured sake for Kan.

"You can say that again. You don't need a knife to kill a construction worker."

The party of four never got off the ground and broke up with half of the sake left. On the way out, Akiyuki stopped in at the boss's house for a glass of water. The boss was doing accounts in the six-mat room with the wooden floor that served as his office. Next to him his son was watching television with the sound turned down.

"I want you to make a little phone call for me," said Mie to Akiyuki.

Mie's face looked entirely different from the one she had been showing her mother. All at once it was etched with illness and exhaustion.

"Tell Yoshiko about the memorial service for Daddy. Mother and I have done everything, so tell her to come like we planned. Please Akiyuki, don't tell her I'm sick. If she asks why I don't come to the phone myself, tell her I caught a cold and I'm wearing a surgical mask."

"Wearing a mask?" he laughed.

"I don't want to worry her. She's been looking forward to it."

Mie promised she would be better by the memorial service. Whenever the mother or Mie mentioned the word "father" in connection with the memorial service, Akiyuki briefly concluded that he was one of the family, too, but then he'd become flustered when he realized his mistake. Afterward, he thought of the man. How could he be his father? It gave him a bad feeling, made him ill. He mused. He just wanted to rub things out, make them pure as if they had never been, the way you crush a blade of grass under your heel. What had the man thought about him all these years? Akiyuki looked just like his father. Sometimes it occurred to him that through his veins, too, ran the same sensuous blood that would make him chase a woman whether she was a widow with children, a whore, or a proper young woman. He'd kick someone when they were down. Betray his friends. Take advantage of another's weaknesses. Where had that man come from? He had an office in the business district. In one generation he'd become a big property owner. The rumor was that he was taking a cut from all the land brokers. Akiyuki would occasionally hear these rumors, and he would think to himself that the man was just a small-time crook.

Once, when he was going to pick up cement with Yasuo, Akiyuki had run into the man. At first he didn't notice him.

"It's no good, I'm feeling shaky, 'cause Mitsuko's squeezing me dry." Yasuo was apologizing. Akiyuki's strength was of a different order from Yasuo's. To him a bag of cement was light as a feather. The man's eyes were fixed on him. He was sitting astride a ridiculously huge motorcycle, the kind ridden by seventeen- or eighteen-year-old street toughs. And though he didn't do any actual construction work, he was wearing the work breeches and the tinted sunglasses. No matter how you looked at him, he was a big man.

"Whadda you want? You got business with me?" Akiyuki said. "I'm not some freak. Fuck off."

The man sat quietly but didn't move. The roar of his engine was deafening.

That evening, Yoshiko called the mother from Nagoya. They were about to set off in the truck that belonged to the store.

It was already one in the morning when the canvas-topped truck arrived. At the sound of the horn, Akiyuki came outside. The children were struggling to jump down from the flatbed area in the rear. "Hey, I told you they'd be awake," said the boy catching sight of him. The little girl stuck her head out.

"Hurry up and jump down," she said.

"Don't push me," said the boy.

The lights went off and the engine died. The driver's door swung open with a creak and the brother-in-law got out. "We're here, we're here!" He greeted Akiyuki, and then opened the door to the passenger's seat.

"Yoshiko, Yoshiko, we're here. She's dead asleep," he laughed. "Yoshiko, we're in Kishū, home of your beloved mother."

The two children jumped down from the truck at the same time.

"She's been excited for months. 'We're going to Kishū, we're going to Kishū,' she kept saying, but now that we're finally here, she's asleep." The brother-in-law spoke loud in amazement.

"Hey, you two, this... is Kishū."

At the sound of his voice, three-year-old Hisashi, asleep with his hand on Yoshiko's breast, woke up. Looking embarrassed at having been caught napping, he tapped his mother on the cheek, saying, "Kishū, Kishū." Finally, Yoshiko opened her eyes. Seeing Akiyuki standing before her she said, "Oh, we're in Kishū," and got out of the truck.

"I was dreaming. Somewhere along the way, I was about to tell you to stop so I could sleep in the mattress in back, but then I fell fast asleep."

"You always sleep in the car," said the boy.

"It felt wonderful. Your dad was saying, 'Yoshiko, we're crossing Yanoko Pass,' and I heard him, but I couldn't open my eyes. I can't really remember, but I was having a good dream, a happy dream."

"Yoshiko, You're always happy about Kishū." The brother-in-law's voice reverberated in the night.

The brother-in-law held the little boy, who was fussing because he felt sleepy again. Leaving the truck as it was, they went into the house.

The mother and stepfather were waiting for them.

"Welcome, welcome," said the mother, looking the Nagoya family over and then spreading out a futon in the TV room for Hisashi, who had fallen asleep in his father's arms, "You're so late, I was worried."

Yoshiko laughed.

"All those mountain roads. And nothing to look at but those dark mountains. Every time I come here, it scares me, it's so far out in the sticks." Yoshiko addressed this comment to the mother and then, assuming a humble expression and pressing her hands together in greeting, turned to the stepfather, who was in his long underwear.

"I'm afraid we haven't been able to prepare much," said the stepfather.

"Just go get into Hisashi's futon," the brother-in-law ordered the children, who were complaining that they were sleepy. The brother-in-law stood where he was and bowed his head. He didn't seem to know how to greet his relatives.

"Want a beer?" Akiyuki asked him.

"Sure," said Yoshiko, answering for her husband.

Yoshiko took off her dress. Then she asked her husband to spread out futons for the two older children, who continued to whine at her.

"Oh, I'm beat from riding in that old heap of junk with Hisashi climbing all over me" She stretched her neck from side to side. "My shoulders are stiff," she said to Akiyuki. And then to her husband, "Later, give me a backrub."

"I can't believe you, child, when your husband's the one exhausted from all the driving." the mother looked truly amazed. "You're almost forty but you're still acting like a drill sergeant, just the way you used to. You should act more wifely."

"How can I act like a wife when I've got kids hanging all over me?" Yoshiko took one of the stepfather's cigarettes from the top of the cabinet and lit it. Blowing a long trail of smoke through her nose, she looked over at Akiyuki.

"Akiyuki, you look more and more like your older brother," she said. "Have you grown? No wonder Mie kept mentioning it on the phone."

The stepfather tactfully withdrew into the parents' own room in the interior part of the house, saying he had accounts to finish up. Akiyuki got some beer out of the refrigerator. The mother kept an eye on him, as the normally empty refrigerator was now stuffed with ingredients for the memorial ceremony meal.

"I don't know when we crossed Yanoko Pass. I could hear Papa saying, 'We're at the pass,' but then I dozed off, and when they finally woke me up and I looked around, there was Akiyuki. Mother and Akiyuki." Yoshiko scratched at her arms. She had red marks on her skin.

"There can't be any bugs in that truck," laughed the brother-in-law.

"It itches like crazy," Yoshiko said and then suddenly lowered her voice. "I crossed that same pass once all by myself. Carrying a bundle with all my things. I had Brother come halfway to see me off, let's see, I was fifteen and he was sixteen. Now looking back on it, I was just a baby. I took the train to Kinomoto, got a bus to go over the pass, and then hopped on another train to Owase. Even now I remember clearly—I had a little time with Brother before the bus left, so we ate noodles with sweet tofu in front of the station. He was so full of life then," Yoshiko reminisced. "Brother asked me, 'Do you want some noodles?' I didn't want him to think I was afraid, so I ate a whole bowl down to the last drop of broth. I said good-bye to him and got on the bus. After Yanoko Pass, I don't know why, but I cried and cried even though I didn't feel sad or so bad off."

"Akiyuki was still small, and Mie wasn't well you know," said the mother apologetically.

"This kind of talk is Yoshiko's specialty," said the brother-in-law.

"It comes back to me all the time. The other day when I went to the coffee shop near our house, there was a girl there, a factory worker or something. She was always sitting there looking glum, but this time she'd dyed her hair red and I couldn't believe how pretty she looked. Papa said, 'Oh, another nice girl gone bad,' but to me she felt like my little sister and I was happy for her."

"The factories are bad enough but the cotton mills are even worse," said the brother-in-law. "How old was that girl, sixteen or seventeen?"

Yoshiko nodded. She scratched her arm again.

"Be happy. Look pretty, make money, and don't do anything stupid. You're no stranger to me. That's what my heart was saying. But after that she didn't come around again."

"Come to think of it, when I started school you were the one who sent me a knapsack," Akiyuki said.

"Not only a knapsack. Clothes and shoes too," Yoshiko said turning to the mother. The mother nodded.

"Every month without fail I got a letter from Mother. Mother can't write so well, so she had someone do it for her and the letters were full of difficult words. I couldn't read them myself so I had someone in the dorm read them for me. I can still remember those letters: 'Dear Yoshiko, it's the end of autumn, how are you?' But they all boiled down to one thing: send money. It was so embarrassing. Whenever I got a letter, I'd send money right away without having my dorm friends read it to me. If I ignored the letter and didn't send money, I'd get a telegram: Mother in critical condition, Brother in critical condition, Mie in critical condition."

"What else could I do? I was a woman alone, and your brother barely ever came home."

"I know. I know, but it would take me by surprise. Mie wasn't well so when I got a telegram like that in the middle of the night, it gave me a shock. I came home twice. Fooled by my own mother," laughed Yoshiko. She trembled beneath her slip.

"The only time it was real was when Brother killed himself."

They finished off five bottles of beer, and while Akiyuki went to get more the mother took a moment to give the couple from Nagoya an account of the murder that had occurred among Mie's in-laws. Yoshiko couldn't believe it. The funeral at the house by the beach had only been two weeks ago, and Akiyuki, too, felt he had been tricked by some malevolent spirit. Even those close to the people involved couldn't comprehend what had happened.

"Poor thing," said Yoshiko sipping her beer.

"Fire and murder—our local specialties," Akiyuki said. The mother stared at him. You could probably find reasons for each fire or murder, if you looked carefully enough, but the real reason was the land itself, hemmed in by mountains and rivers and the sea and steaming in the sun. People went crazy fast.

"Mie's laid up," the mother revealed.

"I had no idea. She's in bed?"

"You know how she is. She could have left it alone, it's their mess after all, but she acted like she was one of them—like one of her own family had done it—and she ran herself into the ground. She should have just left it alone, but no . . . Mitsuko and Yasuo are good-for-nothings, and as for Furuichi, I bet he deserved it."

"Yasuo, you say, you mean that Yasuo?"

"Supposedly a sailor, but really a gangster."

"And Mitsuko, you mean that Mitsuko?"

The mother nodded.

"The last I heard of her, she'd run off with a truck driver or a sailor, they said. Abandoned her kids."

"She came back. But then she sent the kids away."

"There's a lot of talk about that woman. Just like me in the old days," said Yoshiko, looking at the brother-in-law. "I couldn't believe it when I heard she'd run off leaving a nursing baby, and then how Mie's husband beat some sense into her. I'd never do that if it were me. Hey, Papa, if I get serious with another guy, I won't leave you with the kids. They'll come with me and my lover. Don't worry!"

Yoshiko opened her suitcase. Inside was a kimono wrapped in Japanese paper.

"What do you think, Mother?" she said triumphantly, "I may be poor but I'm not going to wear some old thing to Daddy's memorial service. These occasions hardly ever come along, so I said the hell with it and had this made."

"Very nice," the mother nodded.

"I'm his daughter, I can't wear any old rag. And besides, I'm the eldest."

Yoshiko stood up in her slip and held the kimono against her.

On the morning of the memorial service, the children from Nagoya were up early horsing around. Akiyuki felt sluggish, probably from drinking beer and going right to sleep. The sun poured in. He did twenty push-ups and twenty sit-ups in his underwear. He'd taken the day off work, but he didn't expect there would be anything for him to do. His mother, his sisters, and the women in the neighborhood were taking care of preparations for the meal after the ceremony, which would take place in the house where the mother now lived. Yoshiko had been against it. And she had a point—it was strange. The house was the mother's and the stepfather's. But it really belonged to the stepfather. Yet they were holding a memorial service for the mother's former husband there. What did the stepfather think about it?

The oldest girl peeped in timidly. "If you're up, it's breakfast time," she said gravely.

From the main house, Yoshiko yelled, "Akiyuki, chow!"

Her voice sounded oddly like the mother's. Akiyuki grunted a reply, and when he emerged in his underwear, Yoshiko laughed, saying, "Letting that big thing swing in the wind, you should be ashamed of yourself. Put some clothes on."

"Isn't he ashamed?" Yoshiko asked the mother.

"He doesn't know what shame is."

The mother took out Akiyuki's everyday clothes. Normally she would be giving him his work clothes.

"When Akiyuki and Fumiaki take a bath they walk around naked until I tell them to put on some underwear because they'll embarrass themselves if somebody stops by."

"You're surrounded by cavemen."

While Akiyuki was eating, Fumiaki appeared. Catching sight of him, the stepfather scolded, "You better get up earlier. You say you want to live in an apartment, but I'm not going to let you do it just so you can stay out late."

"We were digging yesterday," said Fumiaki. "It tires me out no matter what."

"You'd be fine if you went to bed early. You can't get up because you're out all night," said the stepfather.

"Tough, isn't it," said the brother-in-law.

"My father's always on at me. Even on the site, he's ragging on me," said Fumiaki swallowing the mother's food with a look of distaste.

"You think I do it because I like to? It's because you make me."

"How old are you, Fumiaki?" asked Yoshiko.

"Twenty-six. Two years older than me," Akiyuki answered.

Fumiaki nodded, his mouth full.

With the sister from Nagoya and her three kids, Akiyuki went to the boss's house. The sun was blazing, bathing all the houses and trees in light. Day after day he walked this same road. Seeing the sun high in the sky made him feel guilty for taking a day off from work. But as he watched the three children running and chatting, yelling excitedly at each other, he reminded himself that this was a special day.

"Akiyuki, you've really grown," said Yoshiko.

Without the makeup she had been wearing the night before, Yoshiko suddenly looked older.

"Seeing how big you've grown, and walking down this road, I feel like I'm dreaming. Everything's a dream."

"You've gotten older, sister."

"That's life. I got three kids you know. All of this is in my past. In the old days, it was all rice fields around here. I used to get in fights around the neighborhood, and Mother and Brother would look appalled. Yoshiko, act more like a girl, they'd tell me."

The children had already entered the boss's house. Pasting a smile on her face, Yoshiko announced dramatically, "Oh, Mie, it's your big sister come from Nagoya."

Yoshiko went inside. Akiyuki followed. They could hear Mie. She sounded hoarse and weak.

Yoshiko placed a box of jellies by Mie's pillow and sat down. "What a terrible thing," she said.

Mie sat up with a smile that was more like a grimace. She pulled together the front of her nightgown. In only a day she looked utterly changed. Her hair was tangled, and her face now had a dark blue tinge.

"I'm losing my voice and I don't feel too good. I thought I could get better before Daddy's memorial service, but I'm not going to make it."

Mie seemed to have shrunk since the day before.

"Pleurisy, they told you? The quacks around here feed you a line even when they don't have a clue," said Yoshiko. Then to the children roughhousing in the next room, she yelled, "Pipe down in there. Akiko, your aunt's sick and I want to have a quiet talk with her. Take Hisashi and go buy some candy at the store."

"Mom," hushed the girl as she came toward them. "We've been there already. There was this scary old man in front of the store.

He looked like a beggar, with a black face and goggly eyes. He asked us where we came from, and when I told him, I don't know, it's none of your business, he showed me this horrible hand and said, 'I'm going to use this to cut you up and eat you.'"

"Uncle Gen," Akiyuki said.

"Hisashi howled so we ran away."

"There's nothing to be frightened of," said Mie. With her hoarse voice, she sounded as if she were singing. "He might be our uncle, but there's something uncanny about him," she laughed weakly.

"He was scary," said Hisashi, coiling himself around Yoshiko's knees. "I cried."

"Crybaby," Akiyuki teased. "Why didn't you give him a big punch in the nose?"

He poked Hisashi in the forehead and the boy, not sure whether he should cry or not, looked over at his mother. Yoshiko didn't respond. Suddenly Hisashi flew at Akiyuki, kicking. Akiyuki dodged.

"Crybaby. Kids from Nagoya just don't cut it. The kids in Kishū are stronger."

Hisashi jumped him. Then he started pounding him on the head wildly.

"O.K., you're strong, you're strong. Nagoya is strong, too," Akiyuki said, "You're not a crybaby, you're not a wimp, you're strong, you're strong."

☙

The memorial service was scheduled to begin at seven o'clock. Mie was sitting in the stepfather's office. In the kitchen the mother and Yoshiko were talking with the hired help and the neighbors. Their voices spilled through the carved transoms above the closed sliding doors. The black kimono suited Mie well, Akiyuki thought. With her hair combed and her makeup done lightly, she looked more like their father than any of them. The stepfather and Fumiaki talked together. The children were being rambunctious.

"Are you feeling bad?" Akiyuki asked.

When she tried to answer, her voice broke, so she simply shook her head. Then she stared at him.

Finding her gaze oppressive, Akiyuki went to the kitchen. Yoshiko, whose kimono made her look even older, was talking to the mother.

"Is Mie lying down?" asked the mother, "She's so pale, and I'm worried that if she's up and around she'll tire herself out and get sick again."

While the mother was talking, the guests arrived, a mixture of the stepfather's relatives, the workers in the stepfather's crew, and neighbors. The priest popped into the kitchen unexpectedly. "You've become quite the lady," he said to Yoshiko

Yoshiko's expression instantly changed to a smile.

"I feel so happy. To have our very own priest at Father's service."

"I was wondering who it was. Just as I was saying, I know that face, it turns out to be little Yoshiko. But you've grown up, haven't you."

"I'm an old lady already."

"No, no, it's just that I've known you since you were this small. And you went through a lot... isn't that right, Mother?"

"It's the same for everybody," said the mother gruffly.

At a loss, the priest said, "We'll talk more later," and headed toward the room with the family altar. The stepfather, Fumiaki, the boss, and the brother-in-law would all be gathering there.

"Afterward, please have some sake," said Yoshiko.

The priest looked back and nodded.

"I'm so happy our priest is here. Daddy would be happy, too. Right, Mother, what could be better?" Yoshiko sounded tearful. "It means so much more to me...instead of having some big-time priest, we've got our own priest who used to read the sutras for us at our little altar when we were kids, even if we couldn't make an offering."

The mother and Yoshiko were just discussing how they would wait ten minutes more and then begin the service when a voice sounded outside.

"Mie, Mie," the voice called.

After a moment they realized it was Uncle Gen.

"Mie, Mie, are you here? It's your Uncle Gen," the voice was saying.

Yoshiko suddenly went silent.

"It's Uncle Gen," Akiyuki said. He peered out of the kitchen window. It wasn't completely dark yet. But he couldn't tell where the loud voice was coming from. The mother scowled.

"I can't tell where he is," he said. "He's invisible, like a ghost."

"Don't pay any attention," said the mother.

"Uncle!" Yoshiko called, coming to stand next to Akiyuki. There was no answer. Yoshiko's hand rested on Akiyuki's shoulder. He could smell her makeup.

"Go fetch him," Yoshiko said, realizing that her summons had failed.

Uncle Gen was standing by the tool shed yelling, "Mie, Mie." He was drunk again. When Akiyuki grabbed him by the arm, Uncle Gen shook him off. "Hey young man, excuse me. I may not amount to much but I'm still your uncle. Bring me sake, sake."

"There's plenty in the house," he said. "Yoshiko's here from Nagoya."

"Oh, so Yoshiko's here, too." Uncle Gen plunged his hands

into his pockets, and almost lost his balance. "She wouldn't forget her father's service now, would she?"

Akiyuki took Uncle Gen by the arm. Again he was shaken off. Slowly, Gen raised his hand over his head. "Look. Scary, huh?"

"What? Doesn't bother me."

Akiyuki led him to the doorway. But Gen just stood there calling out, "Mie, Mie." No matter what was said to him, Uncle Gen wouldn't go in the house.

Akiyuki saw that Mie had slid open an inner door and was walking out unsteadily. She settled herself near the kitchen.

"So, Uncle, am I to understand you're here for the memorial service?" said Yoshiko.

"Yoshiko, greet your uncle properly. Bring me sake, sake. I don't like bad people. Bad people always get what's coming to them in the end."

Yoshiko gestured for Akiyuki to bring some sake. From behind the mother advised, "You don't have to."

Uncle Gen was weaving back and forth. He sat down on the raised step in the entryway.

"What business do you have here?" the mother shouted from behind Akiyuki. Yoshiko turned around. "You're no relation of ours. How could we stand being related to a bum like you? Go home!" shouted the mother. "Go home, or I'll throw you out."

Akiyuki grabbed the mother by her sleeve. Yoshiko stared at her. "Easy does it, Mother," she whispered.

"What do you mean 'easy'? I never got a scrap of food from that bunch. When we were poor, they were doing great, but they never even gave us the time of day. Who calls him 'Uncle'? Mie and Yoshiko don't have an uncle."

"Even so, he is our uncle," said Yoshiko, her eyes filling with tears.

"'Uncle'—Hmmph. These days he comes around sweet talking

you with all this uncle stuff, but then he sponges money and sake from Mie, who's far too generous. Well, it won't work here. Go home."

Uncle Gen sat down on the step, seemingly deaf to the mother's words, calling "Mie, Mie," in a soft, pitiful voice. A neighbor's face appeared in the entryway and quickly withdrew. Finally the stepfather emerged from the interior.

"What's all this shouting in front of my house. It's a disgrace. What do you want?" he demanded.

Mie, who until that moment had been near the kitchen, got up unsteadily and moved toward the back of the house. Suddenly, there was a crash, the sound of glass shattering in one of the back rooms.

"Let me go," a shrill voice sounded. "Get off me!"

Mie was screaming.

The mother and Akiyuki rushed back to the room with the family altar.

"Mie!" the mother exclaimed.

The boss had her pinned from behind, and she was twisting her head back trying to bite him on the arm. The assembled guests were all taking cover in the corners of the room. The sister had apparently knocked over the family altar, as Buddhist implements were scattered all over and fruit was rolling about on the floor.

"Mie, what are you doing? Mie!" said the boss.

Mie was emitting little animal cries and struggling to loosen the boss's grip. The mother sank down.

"Mie, Mie," the mother said.

"Kill me, kill me!" Mie screamed, twisting her head.

They put Mie, still struggling, in the car between Akiyuki and Yoshiko and had Fumiaki take them to her house. Fumiaki went back by himself, leaving only the three of them—Akiyuki and his two sisters—in the house. Nobody else was there. Even though she was in her own home, Mie trembled, saying that someone was coming to kill her. Akiyuki and Yoshiko stayed with their frightened sister.

The memorial service, so eagerly anticipated by the two sisters, was now going on without them at the stepfather's house.

Mie burrowed down into the futon, and curled herself up, almost like she was playing a game of hide-and-seek. "I'm so frightened, I'm so frightened," she repeated.

"Mie," said Yoshiko, "what are you saying? Try to pull yourself together." She stroked the futon.

Akiyuki heard a passing train. Clattering along the rails, it was headed from the station toward the steel bridge. He listened to the sound until it died away.

When Mie heard Uncle Gen calling her at the stepfather's house, she thought her own father had appeared. Mie, who more than anyone felt a bond with the deformed Uncle Gen and even feared him, had heard her father calling her through her uncle's voice. This was the house where the father had lived and died and the brother had hanged himself. They should have held the memorial service to calm the dead here.

"I'm so frightened, I'm so frightened."

Akiyuki looked over at Yoshiko, who was comforting her sister as she lay curled up in the futon. If the spirits of the dead really do exist, let them appear now and comfort Mie and Yoshiko. Let them comfort Mother.

He remembered the other time Mother had gotten angry and

told someone to get lost in just the same way. That time with his elder brother.

"You want me to kill you!" the brother had said.

The mother hadn't hesitated. "If you want to, go ahead, just do it. I gave birth to you and wore myself to the bone raising you, and now that I want to take things a little easier, you want to kill me!"

And then, once the brother had lost the urge to stab them, or even wave his knife in the air, and was gradually sobering up, she chased him off saying, "You're no child of mine. I won't have you ruining your life here where I can see it. If you're really such a big man, go get yourself a woman in town and set up somewhere in some workers' digs."

The memory of his mother at that moment had stayed with Akiyuki. After the brother had left, the mother broke down. He couldn't make out the words in his stepfather's deep voice, but then he heard his mother sobbing, drawing out the syllables, "It's all my fault."

She sounded completely different from just a few minutes before.

"It's my fault. I've done too many bad things."

He could hear her even though he had covered his ears.

It's all Brother's fault, he's the bad one, not you Mother, he thought, his body shaking as his mother sobbed, his heart about to break, curled up helplessly in his futon. The two adults were discussing whether they should separate or not. Akiyuki wept. If his mother and stepfather split up, he didn't feel he could live. From the next futon, Fumiaki reached out his hand and began stroking his head. Akiyuki felt his body brimming over with sadness and anxiety. Fumiaki stuck his own head under the covers saying, "Don't cry."

In the house that morning, with the rain shutters tightly closed, Akiyuki felt that Fumiaki's hand in his had narrowly rescued them all. In this house the stepfather and the mother and their two children had always lived that way—linking hands to warm each other and to shelter each other from the outside world. But the mother had nonetheless rejected both the brother and Uncle Gen. And that wasn't all. She had rejected the man who was his natural father.

"I'm so frightened, so frightened," said Mie. Every time she spoke, the covers moved up and down.

"You've got to get control of yourself," was all Yoshiko could muster. Akiyuki could hear the night insects humming.

The glass front door to the boss's house was still open. Akiyuki got up and closed it. At the sound of his footsteps on the tatami, Mie said, "They're here, they're here."

"You're crazy," he said.

If anyone could comfort her, he would welcome them. But if anyone came to torment or harass her, he would kill them with his bare hands. Suddenly, Mie burst into tears. Yoshiko was rubbing her back when she began to call hoarsely, "Mother, Mother," twisting her head and gripping the futon cover with both hands.

"Mother's not here. I want to go to her place," she said.

Yoshiko was stroking Mie's back. "That woman..." She covered her face with her hands. "She's no mother."

"Mother, Mother!" Mie grew more agitated.

"How can you call her Mother! What did that woman ever do for us?" said Yoshiko.

Akiyuki was staring at the two sisters.

"If she's going to be a mother, she should act more like a mother."

For three days after the memorial service—until the family from Nagoya went home in their canvas-topped truck—Mie clung to them all as if she were a child again. She ran a slight fever. But

she refused to lie down. I'm better, she insisted. It was as if somewhere in her body something had come undone. She'd burst into
tears or shake with fear. The boss was at a loss. "Take off from
work and stay close to her," he ordered Akiyuki.

Sometimes the changes in Mie would make them laugh. At
one point Mie had asked Yoshiko to reminisce about the past.
Yoshiko spoke, and just as her story was getting interesting, Mie
tearfully blurted out, "I want my mother." Her eyes filled with
tears. "I want to go to Mother's house," she sniffled like a child.
When they tried to dissuade her by saying that the mother was
busy with laundry or cleaning, she wouldn't listen. So Akiyuki
and Yoshiko took their sister—bent over and wobbly on her
feet—to the stepfather's house. The sight of the mother's face
reassured Mie. She lay down on the futon that the mother had
spread out for her. Then she buried her face in the covers, and
she, who until a few moments ago had looked exhausted from
mental and physical strain and from illness, and who had worn
a tearful, hopeless expression, now laughed sweetly.

"Mother smells like grilled eggs."

"You silly," Akiyuki laughed.

Drawn in, Yoshiko laughed too. The mother alone looked
uneasy.

Was Mie playing a trick on them? Akiyuki wondered.
Pretending to go crazy so she could enjoy herself as a child
again?

Mie snatched the hat from the head of Yoshiko's daughter and
placed it on her own head.

The girl suspected that all these laughing adults must be crazy.
"I want to go home," she said

"We should have the doctor look at her as soon as possible,"
the mother said.

"You mean the mountain doctor?" Akiyuki asked.

"No!" Mie suddenly shrieked.

The "mountain doctor" referred to the mental hospital.

"At least you must let the doctor take a look at you."

"Are you trying to kill another child!" screamed Mie.

She got up trying to rush at the mother.

"Mie!" Yoshiko cried and held on to her.

The mother was breathing unevenly.

"Mie, Mie," Yoshiko said softly into her sister's ear. But her sister couldn't hear her.

"Are you trying to kill again? I won't let you get away with it. Murderer! I hate you!"

Mie tried to shake herself free. But now Yoshiko was holding her around the waist.

"I hate you, I hate you! I don't care what happens now, I hate you, I hate you," she gasped.

The mother stared at her. But there were no tears in her eyes.

Mie grew more and more nervous and insisted that they all leave together. So, as the sun set, the mother with Yoshiko and her husband and children escorted Mie home. Mie had spent her married life with the boss in that house, but it was also the house where the dead father and brother had lived. Akiyuki stayed behind. Anger gripped him. He went outside. Where had the breakdown started, he wondered. Usually he went to bed at night, woke with the sun, and went to work. But somewhere along the way that rhythm had been disrupted. He hadn't done it; other people had. Everything was all upside down. The dead are the dead. The living are the living. What did it mean to have a dead father, a dead brother?

☙

The wind was blowing. The air filled with the scent of cold earth.

Akiyuki came to the red-light district. He was in a narrow alleyway. Turning a corner by a bare street lamp, he emerged at the back end of the district. A man and a woman were there. The woman was squatting and holding on to the man's body. When they became aware of his presence, they hurriedly embraced. Just as he was going past them, the woman snickered. He passed the first corner and then, making a big circle, turned a corner that led back to the first alleyway. He could still hear the laughter of the woman.

"Hey, man, how 'bout it? I'll give you a bargain."

A woman smelling of makeup took his arm. Without a word he forcefully shook her off.

"What's your fucking problem, acting like that," cursed the woman. Not wanting to hear any more, he opened the door to the bar Yayoi.

It was a dark place. There were about four booths. As if to make up for the surroundings, a peach-colored light hung down from the ceiling. Behind a counter stood a woman of about sixty.

"Welcome," called the old woman. "Kumi-chan, a customer."

A young woman who had been sitting in a booth with another man stood up. The old woman winked at her.

"Hey, what's going on? Don't be so cruel now," said the customer.

"Don't worry. I'm an old pro. I'll take good care of you," assured the old woman.

"No way," said the man, "Think of your age."

"What are you talking about? I was the best of them all. They were lining up in front of the Yayoi just to have a go with me."

"Yeah, and when was that?"

The young woman took Akiyuki's arm as he stood there. They sat down in a booth in the back.

"What'll you have? Beer, whiskey?"

"Whiskey," he answered.

"That'll cost you," the woman said.

He nodded. And then he stared at her. Under his gaze, she tilted her head.

"What is it?" she demanded. "Don't you like the way I look?"

He shook his head at her. The woman didn't resemble anyone. She stood up, went to the counter, and brought back two whiskeys and water. She rested her hand on his knee. "Are you ticklish?" she said, rubbing his knee with her fingers. He could feel the warmth of her hand.

"Let me touch you a little. If we drag this out too long, Mother'll get mad," the woman said as she caressed his penis through his pants. She continued for a while.

"What? It's still soft," she said. "Come here, give me a kiss."

She put her arms around his neck. "Relax," she said and pulled him closer. Her lips touched his. The woman's tongue darted in between the spaces in his teeth. It moved in his mouth. Then she pulled away.

"Touch me here," she said pointing to her breast. Again she placed her lips on his.

"What, it's still not working," she said.

He nodded. She unzipped his pants. The woman slid her hand inside. Little by little he felt his penis stiffen. "There now," said the woman. He touched her breast. The nipple was hard.

What had he come here to do, he wondered. The woman played with him and then instructed him to put his hand up her skirt. She leaned over and whispered, "There's a room upstairs."

"Forget it," he said.

"You're a strange one," the woman said.

He brushed her hand away. Then for a moment he stared at her. Growing angry, perhaps because he had brushed away her hand, she stood up. "What is it with you? You making fun of me? Or did you just come to bother me when I'm working?"

He grabbed her by the arm and made her sit down.

"I have to ask you something," he said.

"Listen, I'm busy. I've got to make a living here. If you want to talk, talk to Mother."

The woman stood up, bumping her head on the peach-colored light.

"Hey, Mother," she called. "This guy says he wants to talk. If you're free, talk to him, would you?"

"I'm busy right now," replied the old woman without missing a beat. "Tell him we can talk next time."

He left the bar feeling they had chased him out. The woman's name was Kumi. Was she the man's latest mistress? Or was she his child by a whore? Could she also be his younger sister? Questions haunted him. Had the sister fondled her own brother's penis without knowing it, and had she made her own brother touch her breasts? Mentally he asked her: Why are you working in that kind of place? Why the thinly disguised prostitution? He, the man's son, was getting along fine. The man's other daughter, born to the proper young woman, was now a coddled girl herself. But you alone, the child of the whore, how did you end up this way? Or, if the rumors are true, why are you now the man's mistress? His eyes suddenly teared up. He took the long way back and walked along the railroad tracks.

When she saw his face, Yoshiko asked, "Where have you been?"

Because he had been walking through the darkness, the lights of the boss's house blinded him.

"Mie kept calling, 'Akiyuki, Akiyuki,' as if you were her lover or something."

"Tomorrow, take your sister and go to the cape," said the mother.

He stared at her.

"We'll all go to the cape together just like the old days," said

Mie. "We'll all go, won't we. Akiyuki, we'll have a picnic." She tapped on a fake straw-patterned plastic basket that she was holding close to her chest.

"Don't get too excited and overdo it or you'll get a fever again."

"I'm not a baby. I could say the same for you, Mother," said Mie.

Yoshiko laughed at her choice of words.

"Even when you were little, you were weak and high strung and you got upset easily. All I've done is worry about you."

"I'm fine. The pleurisy is gone," said Mie, sharply tapping the plastic basket again. It looked like something a fourteen- or -fifteen-year-old girl would carry.

"I'm counting on you, Akiyuki," said the boss from his office, "...and on you, too," he added to the brother-in-law.

"You mean you're not coming?" Akiyuki asked.

The boss lifted his head.

"What with Furuichi and then with Mie getting sick like this, work is all screwed up. The crew doesn't even know what's going on."

"I've been off too."

"Nothing to do about that. We've been nothing but trouble to you."

The mother, Yoshiko, and the brother-in-law were arranged around the futon where Mie was sitting up. Akiyuki was there. So was the boss. Yoshiko's three kids and Mie's son were upstairs. Akiyuki studied the brother-in-law, who sat there with a vacant look. It must be hard for him to even grasp how they were all connected to each other by blood. It was a strange bloodline, he thought. His sister wasn't the only odd one; the bloodline itself was off. Polluted. Just the sight of his sister clowning around he found ominous.

"Put some grilled egg in for the picnic," said Mie. Turning to Akiyuki she added, "It's delicious. You mix in some sugar and soy sauce with the eggs and cook them on a grill."

"And Mother smells like grilled eggs, does she?" laughed Yoshiko.

"Back when we were poor, grilled eggs was our favorite dish. When Brother and Mie would hear that's what we were having for supper, they cheered."

"Poverty is awful," said the mother.

"Who cares if you're poor," said Yoshiko, "Right, Mie, who cares?"

Her sister didn't answer but rapped sharply on the plastic basket, grinning.

The sun shone down, and in places the brightness was so intense it made the green lawn look black. The trees at the point were waving back and forth in the sea breeze. The treetops bent down, went tall and straight, and bent down again. Except for the trees, nothing blocked the view. There was only an expanse of sea and sky.

The grass tickled Akiyuki as he lay, watching, on his stomach. Mie sat, her shoulders drooping; in her lap she held the plastic basket with the straw pattern. Without makeup, her freckles stood out, and fine lines were visible at the corners of her eyes. Her son and Yoshiko's boy were sumo wrestling with each other as the brother-in-law acted the part of referee. The girl had taken the youngest child, Hisashi, to the gift stand.

Yoshiko had spread a towel on her lap and was peeling fruit. Cutting a piece into four sections, she offered one to Akiyuki and one to Mie. Mie shook her head.

"You've got to eat," said Yoshiko.

Yoshiko stuffed one piece into her own mouth and laid the other on the towel. "Hand me that thermos, will you," she said pointing. It was full of tea. "Now that aluminum foil." It all sounded like too much bother, so Akiyuki deposited the whole picnic bundle in front of her. Yoshiko unwrapped the aluminum foil and started eating a chicken thigh.

"Unlike Mie, I'm not fussy about food. When we were kids, Mother used to praise me for it saying, 'You're a vacuum cleaner.'"

Yoshiko laughed in Akiyuki's direction.

"But she's so critical, once she even called me a vulture." She continued looking at her sister. She gnawed on the chicken.

"Akiyuki, eat up."

He shook his head. It was too tiresome to keep answering Yoshiko.

Suddenly, Mie moaned.

"If only Brother were here, too," she said. Still holding the plastic basket, she got to her feet shakily.

"Akiyuki," said Yoshiko, her mouth full of chicken.

He jumped up quickly and grasped his sister by the hand. Then he pushed her back down. She landed on her bottom in the grass. Even so she managed to keep her grip on the plastic basket.

"If only Brother were here."

"He hanged himself," he said. "He gets a prize for dying first." He stuck out his tongue wanting to make a joke of it.

"Brother is dead," said Yoshiko.

"Oh, we had a great time," exclaimed Mie. Suddenly she wilted. Her shoulders sank even as she clung to the basket.

"But I'm having fun now," she said. "This is fun! The wind is blowing, the sun is shining."

"It's a beautiful day," Yoshiko responded. She winked at Akiyuki.

"You've got to get a hold of yourself."

Mie nodded.

"It's hard, but I'll try my best. You're here, and so is Akiyuki. But I feel weak…like any minute I could come down with pleurisy again."

"Don't be such a coward about it. If you don't get a handle on it, what are we all supposed to do?"

"I'm not strong and I'm afraid of everything but I'll do my best. I have to."

"There, that's a good girl. You know, Mie, I've had a worse time than you. Nowadays I can come home with the whole family to Kishū, but when we announced we were getting married— I've never told this to a living soul—his mother got me by the hair and dragged me all over the tatami. Calling me a trashy slut who had tricked her darling boy. You wouldn't know about such things, you've never been anywhere."

"If only Brother were here."

"Even if Brother had been there, I wouldn't have told him. Many a night I cried myself to sleep."

"It would be fun, if only Brother were here," said Mie.

She narrowed her eyes as if the glare bothered her. The wind from the sea blew relentlessly up the cliff. Because it was a weekday, there were no other people around. The children were racing each other from one corner of the lawn to the other. The brother-in-law had taken Hisashi and gotten into the canvas-topped truck parked over by the gift stand. His sister filled Akiyuki's field of vision. She looked gentle and soft. The spitting image of her own father in the photograph.

"We're having fun, aren't we," said Mie.

They stopped the truck at the grandmother's grave. The cemetery was on top of a cliff overlooking the cape.

They searched for the gravestone, relying on Yoshiko's memory. At last they found it. Instead of incense they offered up a cigarette. Yoshiko, worried that the grandmother might not notice it, burned a piece of paper, too. The flame trembled.

"Granny, are you lonely? You shouldn't be. You see how at least once every decade or so your grandchildren and your great grandchildren come to visit you." Yoshiko spoke out loud so Mie could hear. "Granny put it very well when she came to see us just after Akiyuki was born. 'I won't be lonely because the sparrows and the crows will visit me,' she said."

Yoshiko looked up. "Akiyuki, you idiot!" she yelled. He stood up. "Watch where you put your butt, that's Uncle's grave!"

"Uncle?" he asked.

Mie laughed.

"Mother's older brother, it's his grave," Mie said evenly.

"The mosquitos are eating me alive," said Yoshiko's daughter.

"Let's get going. C'mon, let's go to the whale pool."

"Making us come to the cemetery," scolded Hisashi, running up behind his mother and giving her a kick. His foot landed on Yoshiko's buttocks. Yoshiko instinctively slapped Hisashi on the back with the flat of her hand. The slap resounded. Stung by the pain and the noise, Hisashi's face crumpled, and then, watching the adults' reactions, he began to sniffle. Soon he had brought tears to his eyes and was crying loudly.

"So you think it's O.K. to kick your own parent in the butt?" said Yoshiko. "I'll send you right home to Nagoya."

"You didn't have to hit him so hard," said the brother-in-law stroking Hisashi's head.

"Come on, let's go see the pool," said the little girl to her father.

Only Mie's son was quiet. He stood plucking leaves from wilted flowers in the bamboo vases that adorned the gravestones. "It's so boring here. There's nothing to do. Even the store is just a rip-off."

The girl asked, "Whales? Are there real whales, real live whales in the pool?"

The boy nodded. The girl asked again: "Really? You're not telling stories?"

"Really," the boy finally spoke.

Behind the canvas-topped truck they could see the cape and the sea. Clouds now obscured the sun. Just below the steep cliff that bordered the cemetery grew a forest of bamboo. The wind rippled through the bamboo stalks, bringing out their different hues. Below that was an expanse of grass as far as the eye could see. The tip of the cape, shaped like an arrowhead, protruded into the sea, another stretch of bluish green. Waves beat and splashed up against the black rocks of the cape.

The brother-in-law came and stood next to Akiyuki. "It's a beautiful place," he said.

"There's nothing here," Akiyuki answered.

He wanted to hide the cape from the eyes of his brother-in-law. To make it his own, to prevent anyone else from seeing it. In the old days, the people buried on this mountainside had lived here dependent on rain for drinking water and unable to fish because there was no bay where they could keep a boat, even though they lived but a stone's throw from the water. They had eked out a living cutting fields into the mountainsides. That's what his mother had told him. And when they were no more than children themselves, they would scatter to look after other people's children. His mother had been one of them.

The two sisters were still in the cemetery. The children had climbed into the bed of the truck and were talking about the whale pool where they were going next. To Akiyuki, the two sisters looked much older than their years. Mie was squatting down holding onto the plastic basket that contained the leftovers from the picnic. Yoshiko, bent over slightly, was carefully making her way down a narrow path through the gravestones to a large basin filled with mountain spring water. After filling a rusty, bent tin bucket with water she came staggering back under its weight. Then, using the thermos cup as a scoop, she began to sprinkle water on the gravestones one by one. First the grandmother's grave, then the uncle's grave, then the grave of the child that had died soon after birth. Next she plucked weeds from between the stones. Straining hard, Akiyuki could see the cigarette he had placed there still sending up a faint column of smoke. As he watched his sisters, he wondered if they would just continue on this way as they aged and eventually became old women. He imagined them, old now, cleaning their mother's grave. Talking up a storm. Weeping. Talking would make them happy. Weeping, too. His emotions stirred as he imagined them this way, even though they were not yet old.

"You gonna take forever?" he shouted.

"Just a minute," Mie's voice responded cheerfully.

"If you don't hurry up, I'm gonna leave you here."

"Shame on you," Yoshiko shouted back. "I'm going back to Nagoya and I don't know when I'll be back again, so I'm giving thanks to Granny and Uncle for the old days. And you were the one they spoiled the most! Shame on you."

"I don't know anything about it!" he shouted back.

"Let me die!" Mie ran barefoot out of the house. It was the night after Yoshiko and her family had gone home to Nagoya in their canvas-topped truck. The boss was home at the time. It happened the instant Akiyuki took his eyes off her.

"Akiyuki, get her!" the boss screamed.

Akiyuki flew out of the house after her. Just in front of the railroad crossing, he grabbed her by the back of her collar and pulled with all his strength. She stumbled backward then got up quickly and made as if to push him out of the way. The train had already crossed the steel bridge and was now about to pass them on its way to the station. Mie poised to dive head first in front of it. Akiyuki grabbed her by the hair. She struggled. Still holding on to her by her hair, Akiyuki flipped her over. The boss, who had finally caught up with them, jumped on top of her, pinning her down. He grasped her by the neck and slapped her twice on the cheek hard with his right hand.

"I want to die, I want to die," said Mie kicking her feet. Her skirt rose up. The sight of her white thighs unnerved Akiyuki.

"Let me go, let me go," she cried.

Mie opened her mouth wide and bared her teeth. Twisting her head back and forth, she was trying to bite him. "Fucking crazy!" The boss got astride her again and once more slapped her on the cheek. At that moment a whistle sounded and the train rolled passed them. Breathing hard, Akiyuki felt its roar reverberate through him. The woman who lived next door to the boss stood by, watching.

"I'm going to die, I'm going to die." Mie moaned. The boss remained on top of her, pinning her hands down. He was shirtless, wearing nothing but his long underwear; his muscled arms and legs made him look strangely like an animal.

Akiyuki was filthy. He washed the mud from his bare feet in the bathroom. There in the place where they undressed for the bath he found a plastic whale that must have belonged to Hisashi. Mie moaned on.

"Akiyuki, go get your mother," said the boss.

His feet still wet, Akiyuki slipped on some sandals that probably belonged to the boss. He wanted to save her, he thought, save them all, including himself. But what could he do? Had his sister gone mad? Then he remembered her on that day in the cemetery on the cape. She had looked happy. Only two days had passed since then. And only a few more since her outburst at the memorial service. The changes in his sister didn't seem real. She, who so feared getting sick again, who trembled at the thought of dying, had tried to die.

The mother didn't cry.

"What foolishness," she said.

It was the stepfather who looked stricken. The mother was folding laundry.

"It's bad enough already what with Furuichi dying," said the mother. "I'm going to go over there right away and have a good talk with Mie."

She glanced up at him.

"Go now, you can finish that later," said the stepfather.

But the mother's hands didn't rest.

"It's going to be hard on the boss. What site did you say you're working on now?"

Akiyuki didn't answer. It was too much of an effort to open his mouth.

"Hey," said the mother.

"What?" he answered roughly.

The mother stopped folding the laundry. She stared at him as he stood there.

"Your father asked you a question."

Akiyuki sneered. Then his face crumpled and his eyes filled with tears. What do you mean, 'father'? Don't be an idiot, he wanted to say out loud. I'm not a child anymore. His tears spilled over.

"Akiyuki, you should answer him," said the mother. Her voice was gentle. "I'm going to go over there right now."

Their family was like a house of cards that would topple at the first touch. The family defends itself against enemies. What a lie. And he didn't need a family based on lies. Basically, he didn't need a family at all.

He went to his own room set apart from the house. I'm my mother's child, period. I have no father. He wanted to turn to the mother and demand that she bring back the brother and sister the way they used to be. They were both her children, after all. An image of the man's face came to him. He could hear his voice, too. Yeah, the man meant something to him. But he wasn't going to call him "Father." For god's sake, what kind of mess did you two make? Doing whatever you wanted and making your children pay the price. You're not even human. You're worse than dogs.

If the man were here now, I'd spit in his face. You've been watching me, watching me all the time. Even when I was a child, I could feel your eyes on me. I'll burn them out of their sockets, destroy your gaze. Akiyuki paced around the room. Then he kicked the wall. Even these legs, these arms are full of him.

ॐ

Mitsuko was in the boss's house. A young man stood behind her. When he saw Akiyuki and the mother, he sat down in a formal posture.

"Auntie, I had no idea about Mie," said Mitsuko.

The mother said nothing and sat down by Mie's futon. Seeing the mother, a smile flickered over Mie's face before fading away. She took her hands out of the futon. The left one was bandaged.

"What happened here?" the mother asked.

It was the first time Akiyuki had seen the bandage, too.

"I took my eyes off her for a second and she did it with the razor," said the boss. "I got it away from her, and luckily it was only a flesh wound."

"Auntie, please forgive me—for Yasuo," said Mitsuko.

The young man, realizing that Akiyuki was staring at him, looked away nervously.

"What a stupid thing to do."

The mother was deaf to Mitsuko's entreaties.

"But why did you do it, Mie?" said the mother, taking a deep breath. She exhaled sharply, her shoulders sagging. Mie smiled at her mother again.

"Mie, listen hard. Human beings musn't die. If you die, it's all over. Look at everybody here—they're all alive."

"Forgive me," repeated Mitsuko. She covered her face with her hands. The young man placed a hand on her back. Mitsuko shook him off.

"Stop crying," the boss shouted. "Crying won't do any good." Then he lowered his voice. "What's more important, Mitsuko, is to make sure Yasuo doesn't kill anybody else when he comes out."

Mitsuko nodded.

"It's fine to take in some young guy while Yasuo isn't around, but nobody gets executed these days, so he'll be out again." The boss addressed the young man who was stroking Mitsuko's back. "And you, don't you get too attached to Mitsuko here."

"I understand," the young man nodded.

The hand rested on Mitsuko's back.

"Mie, you musn't talk of dying."

The mother put her hand on Mie's forehead.

"When you got sick with pleurisy, your father and brother prayed so hard that you would live."

"I won't die," said Mie. "I don't want to die."

"Good. You've got to live," the mother removed her hand,

"Just the way your mother, your sister in Nagoya, and Akiyuki are living....Mie, you must not die. I forbid you to even think about it. If an old woman like me can keep on living, how would it look if you died? The gods and buddhas would be shocked. So shocked they'd turn their backs on us for sure. Think about your husband, think about your child."

"I don't want to die. I promise I'll live," Mie repeated hoarsely.

At that moment, Mie looked like a different person from the one who had tried to throw herself under the train. The bandage loomed up strangely white and distinct. Lying there in the futon, she didn't stir. Was she gradually coming to her senses? Akiyuki stared at her. What a strange creature! Was it because she wasn't wearing makeup, or was it the fluorescent lighting that made her face look so pale? She had none of the sensuality that was written all over Mitsuko's face. But that skin, that flesh, those bones—what were they made of? This "strange creature" was none other than his sister who shared a mother with him. It was all so mystifying. Oppressed by his thoughts, Akiyuki rose to his feet. He went to the kitchen and drank a glass of water. The sun was pouring in. He felt he was drinking the sunlight, too.

"Next summer they'll all come from Nagoya again to swim so you must get better."

"If Mie doesn't pull herself through, then I just don't know what I'll do," said Mitsuko, suddenly playing the good girl. The young man stood up. He came into the kitchen. His hair had been permed. As he headed toward the bath, Akiyuki asked him where he was going and he answered, "The toilet."

"Over there," Akiyuki said, pointing in the direction of the front door.

"Jun, darling, what is it?" Mitsuko called.

"The toilet," Akiyuki answered for him.

"He's a man. Tell him to go outside," said Mitsuko.

The young man scratched his head and laughed. With a grin he pointed to the sandals at the back of the kitchen door and asked if he could use them. Akiyuki nodded. There wasn't much difference in height between them. Or in age. The young man had a soft, pretty face like a woman's. But he wouldn't be any match for Yasuo on the crew.

Mie remained in bed. Her face was turned to the side, her hair gathered at the back. The rise and fall of her faintly pink ear made her look like another sort of creature altogether.

"Those kids had so much fun," said the mother sadly. "Kishū is great, they were telling me. They got to see all those live whales in the bay. We want to take them home to Nagoya, they said, and then they started arguing about how the pool in Nagoya just wouldn't work."

"I don't know of any place where they capture whales live and keep them in a bay," said the boss. "This is it."

"You mean Kishū?" Akiyuki mumbled. He remembered the cape projecting out into the sea. The sea was a bluish green.

"I heard that Yoshiko was back from Nagoya, but considering what Yasu did, I just couldn't come to visit. Still, I want to see her. She married into a good Nagoya family, and now she's a proper lady," said Mitsuko. "In the old days, we used to hang around together. . . . When Yoshiko and I were together, even the men couldn't keep up with us, right, boss?"

"Now you're talking shit again."

"Mie's dead brother and the boss were friends. Well, Yoshiko and I weren't friends exactly, but we were close enough. The older brother, the one who died, he was my first love. He was so handsome in a way you'll never be," she said, now addressing the young man. "The barbershop used him as a model." He blushed.

"Don't talk about our brother," Akiyuki said.

"Oh, Akiyuki, you're jealous!" Mitsuko laughed. The mother laughed uncomfortably. Glancing in his direction, Mie smiled faintly.

"Akiyuki's pretty hot, too," said the stepfather, narrowing his eyes, a smirk fixed on his face.

Dirty old fuck, Akiyuki thought. What was coming next?

"There's an office girl who's wasting away with love for Akiyuki, you know. But Akiyuki just ignores her."

"From now on, you've got to watch yourself with women," said the mother.

"How old are you? Twenty-four?" Mitsuko asked.

He nodded but he felt like yelling at them: I'm different from the rest of you with your fucking minds in the sewer.

Outside a voice was calling, "Mie, Mie." It was Uncle Gen. Akiyuki was the first to register it. He glanced at the mother. The voice traveled around from the kitchen door to the front door.

"Mie, are you there? Mie!" the voice called. Now Uncle Gen was standing there. The light was behind him. Instantly, a sense of dread came over Akiyuki. Would his mother start shouting again, he worried.

"She's here, what do you want?" said Akiyuki before anyone else had a chance to speak. Resting his hands on the open door and the door frame to support his weight, Uncle Gen responded, "Tell her her uncle is here." Mie remained silent.

"Don't stand there, come in," Akiyuki said beckoning him.

"Oh, it's Akiyuki?" said Uncle Gen making a silly face.

"You again? What is it this time, more sake?" said the mother.

Trampling on the shoes arranged in the entryway, Uncle Gen stumbled in and sat down noisily on the step up into the house.

"So your mother's here, too?" he asked in a whisper.

"Yeah," Akiyuki nodded.

Uncle Gen reeked of sake.

"Hey there, Mie, get better fast, I've been haggling with the mayor again. I put it to him: Why don't you make this town more convenient? Why didn't you make it rich like other places?"

Here comes another sermon, Akiyuki thought. Uncle Gen waved his right hand.

"You might as well burn it down. What with all these twisty streets wandering all over the damn place, how's a body supposed to get around?"

"You mean stagger around, eh?" the boss teased.

"That's right," laughed Uncle Gen.

Seeing that Akiyuki was now laughing, too, Uncle Gen made a goofy clown face. Could the father have looked like this, Akiyuki wondered. Uncle Gen did resemble the photo of the sisters' father on the small Buddhist family altar in the boss's house. But there were striking differences. Uncle Gen's hair lay in ragged patches on his scalp, as if somebody had gone at it with clippers. His head looked misshapen. Dirt and grime blackened his face. He'd smeared iodine on a cut and now the scab was peeling off. Deep lines creased his forehead. The eyes and teeth were yellow. Someone had either given him clothes or he was wearing his old ones, but they were all patched in places. Who would have mended his clothes? Who would be taking care of him? After Gen had built a shack on city land without permission and the city had razed it, they'd heard nothing about where he was sleeping. People despised and scorned him. But he seemed to take pleasure in it as he bummed his way from one house in the alleyway to the next.

Mie said nothing. She was resting in the futon. Only her ear seemed to signal that she was alive.

"Uncle, Mie has been saying such stupid things. Scold her for me, would you," said the boss.

"O.K.," he nodded, "I'll scold her." Raising his voice, he turned to Mie.

"Hey, you there, Mie, don't do anything stupid. If you do, I'm the one who'll punish you with death. The boss is worried about you. I'll put your ass in jail if you keep this up."

The mother placed her hand on Mie's forehead as if to check her temperature. Tears rose to Mie's eyes and spilled down her cheeks.

"Uncle, you want a drink? We've got some," said the boss.

Akiyuki got up. He opened a beer, and set it and a glass down in front of Uncle Gen.

ৡ

A miniature red bulb had been placed in the fluorescent light fixture that hung down from the ceiling. The light was on. But Akiyuki couldn't see beyond the circle of dim red light. It was humid. He was sweating. The woman looked at him. The two of them were naked.

The woman lay down on top of him. She rubbed her breasts over his chest. She put her hand on his penis saying, "Now, look how big it's gotten. I'll take care of you." Then she tried to put it in. He pushed her off. "Wait a minute," he said.

"You're a strange one. You can have a few minutes but hurry up, O.K? Mother will get pissed off again," said the woman.

Again the woman studied him. She was using his arm as a pillow. With her own hair, she tickled the hair in his armpits. Then she pushed her nose into his armpit and took a deep sniff.

"You don't stink, you smell fresh like soap," whispered the woman as if to herself. "If only I could do it with young guys all the time."

Until a short time ago, Akiyuki had been out walking around town. Telling his mother that he needed to buy new tabi for work the next day, he had left the house. He wanted to be alone. Otherwise he was going to suffocate, he thought. He wanted to get far away from his mother and his sister. Wanted to break free of his brother who had hanged himself from a tree that morning long ago. Soon he emerged at the railroad crossing. The branches of the lone tall tree there were quivering. Who the fuck was he? He was his mother's child and his sister's little brother. But so what? The anxiety gnawed at him. The truth was, he was only related to his sisters on one side. They didn't share a father. Uncle Gen was not his uncle. He could try to hide it or gloss over it, but it was the truth. He walked on. If only he could run into that man. His sister had her dead father, and he had a father, too; like any human being or animal, it had taken a male and a female to create him. That male parent did exist. And he had some unfinished business with him. If he pricked himself with a needle, he felt his skin would rip open and his whole being would drain away. One small nick and he could purge himself of everything. Now his excitement rose. He would commit one terrible crime and get revenge on the man. No, he'd rather be the victim of a terrible crime himself.

He had lost track of his whereabouts.

At some point he came to the shadowy red-light district. Fumes from the pulp factory across the river filled the air. Whenever the smell wafted across the water all the way to the district, it meant rain that night. The weather in this region changed constantly. They were cursed with rain. Nothing good ever came of it. He stopped in front of the bar Yayoi. Should he go in or go straight back home? He hesitated. His heart was pounding. Someone behind him was watching, he could feel it. I'll smash those eyes with a rock, he thought, and pushed open the door.

He went right to the woman, who was sitting to one side, and pulled money out of his pocket.

The woman remembered him. "What?—you scraped some money together to come back?"

Akiyuki told her he wanted to be alone with her.

"O.K.," she said.

"Mother, is the second floor free?"

The old woman at the counter cocked her head. "Well, let me see," she said dramatically, "Just a minute. It looks like somebody went up there a little while ago."

The old woman pushed two buzzers on the counter.

"If it's occupied, Kumi, you can use the Misugi. You're both young so nobody'll take much notice."

The right buzzer rang in response. The left one didn't.

"Is that room free?" the old woman asked. In the peach-colored fluorescent lighting, she looked like a demon.

It was a four-and-a-half-mat room. The rain shutters were closed up tight and curtains hung in the window. The futon was laid out. A sofa and a table sat on a narrow stretch of wooden floor. The woman tugged on the light string. The room turned peach. To Akiyuki it felt like magic. The woman's face looked different now. Her eyes were shining.

"O.K., take off your clothes," she said.

He felt flustered. The sound of a woman's laughter floated down the hall and up the stairs. It was humid. The rain would start any minute, he thought.

The woman took her clothes off down to her panties.

"What're you doing, slowpoke. C'mon, take off your clothes."

Akiyuki remained motionless. He realized that the words wouldn't come. Are you the child of that man? he was asking in his head but he couldn't say it out loud. The room was musty with the scent of men's and women's bodies.

The woman took off her panties.

"Hurry up, take off your clothes, let's have some fun." The woman got into the futon. Thinking he could still postpone things, Akiyuki took off his shirt and his pants. He got into the futon in his underwear. Suddenly, the woman kissed him. She pushed her tongue into his mouth. He trembled. It was his first time. He took off his underwear. The woman touched his erect penis. She encircled him with her thighs. He brushed his face against her breasts and caressed them with his hands. Then he sucked on the woman's hard pointed nipples that sprung up red as if they had a life of their own.

"No, no, don't do that," said the woman, her voice now strangely clear.

He bit down on the nipples softly with his teeth. Had that man been here before him?

"No, no," the woman said again. She twisted her head. He let go of the nipples. They bore red tooth marks. I'm violating the child of that man, he thought. I'm trying to degrade the man himself. No, I'm trying to degrade all who share my blood—my mother, my sister, and my brother, too. Degrade everything. The woman was moaning, her arms around his neck. He thrust his penis deep inside her. She closed her eyes and cried out.

My sister? he asked himself. My long-lost sister through that man? He rubbed his cheek against hers. How I've longed for you. Ever since I was a little boy, I've wondered about you. He ejaculated. The woman looked dazed.

He wanted to make certain he had done it with his sister even though he knew who she was. Animal, beast. It no longer mattered what people called him or how they punished him for it.

The woman pulled at the hair under his arms. It tickled. Putting her mouth to the arm that served as her pillow, she bit down gently and barked, pretending to be a dog. When he didn't respond she said, "What're you thinking about?" Still he didn't answer.

The woman turned over. From a stash that was kept there she took a cigarette, put it in her mouth, lit it, and coughed. "Here," she said and handed it to him. The cigarette was wet with her saliva. He took a drag and gave it back to her, ordering her to put it out.

"What, you don't smoke?" said the woman, still coughing. She stubbed the cigarette out in the ashtray.

"Do you ever think of dying?" he asked.

"Damn, you're really hopeless," the woman said. She wrapped her feet around his. "At my age, why would I think about such things? One of these days I'm going to marry a very rich man. You musn't butt in and say I worked as a prostitute here when the time comes."

He nodded. She reached out for his penis again. A vision came to him of the cape protruding into the sea. Swell up, rise up, he thought. Tear the sea to pieces. She took his swollen penis and began to caress it vigorously.

"It must be tough being a man—having that thing making you sin all the time. Being led around by the nose. "

Suddenly, he embraced the woman.

"Ouch!" she said.

He pushed her down, and got on top. The woman drew up her knees and lifted her hips like a true professional.

"What's the big rush, I said I'd take care of you," said the woman. Then she laughed, acting kittenish and grinding her hips.

"Don't hug me so hard."

This woman was definitely his younger sister, he thought. Their hearts were beating hard. How I've longed for you, their hearts were saying to each other. With his ass in the air like an animal, he didn't know what to do even though she meant so very much to him. He wanted to pluck out his beating heart and press it into her breast, merge their two hearts, rub them one against the other. The woman moaned. Their sweat flowed. I'm your brother. We two are the pure children of that man, the one I can now call "Father" for the first time. If only we had hearts for sex organs. Akiyuki wanted to rip open his chest, and show his sister, her eyes closing as she strained and moaned, the blood of that man running through his veins. From that day on he would smell like an animal. His armpits would stink like Yasuo's. Off in the distance he could hear somebody, perhaps a drunk, yelling. The woman cried out, her eyes tightly shut, as if she couldn't take any more. Beads of sweat stuck to her eyelids like tears. Now, he thought, that man's blood will spill over.

House on Fire

He was a big man. No one had a clue where he'd come from. But it was a small town. They could make a rough guess, mostly from his accent. It sounded like Atawa or Kinomoto, or at the furthest Owase. The man wore khaki pants, a khaki vest, and a hunting cap. The son remembered his mother telling him about the man at some point, but he couldn't remember exactly when. A train had been rumbling past the house.

"Come in," ordered the son's older brother.

The man just stood his ground, spitting into the gully that ran along the barley fields.

"Please, come in," pleaded the brother, now on the verge of tears.

"Naw." The man spit again, then wiped his face with his hand, "Later. I gotta job to do today."

The brother stepped outside. "I'm going with you."

"No, this ain't somethin' I can do with a kid like you."

The man walked toward the station. The brother followed. Cutting through the barley field, the man jumped over a stick fence and the brother followed. They were on the railroad tracks.

"You mean I'd get in your way?" asked the brother as he hopped from one railroad tie to the next.

There was no reply. The sound of the gravel crackling under the man's footsteps grated on the brother's ears. The man was planning to ditch him. A train appeared from the direction of the station. The man jumped aside nimbly, gathering enough momentum to land on the grassy bank opposite. The brother followed.

"I told you not to come, you little shit, get the fuck outta here."

"C'mon, let me join you."

"I'm not that desperate."

"So let me do stuff for you."

"Yeah, that'll get 'em talkin' for sure—me chasing a young widow with her kid in tow."

The man stopped abruptly. He spat, making a whistling sound through the gap in his teeth. It was a habit of his. He had just come back from the war. Or maybe he hadn't gone off to war at all.

"Who cares?" asked the brother, staring at the man. "Let people talk if they want to."

The train whistle sounded.

How old would his older brother have been then? At least eleven or twelve.

A sharp smell of grass filled the air. Not a breath of wind. Pampas grass and wormwood leaves gleamed as if they had shed their outer layers under the hot sun. The mother's first husband had died, and now the brother lived in the house with his three young sisters. Copying the man, the brother whistled through his teeth and spat. He tore off a wormwood leaf and bit down on it. The man moved off again and the brother followed.

Together they cut through the train station to get to Ueda no Hide's house. When Ueda no Hide saw the brother standing behind the man, he laughed. "So you've given up becoming a horse trader?"

Ueda no Hide was carefully wiping the lids of surplus canned

Occupation goods he had picked up somewhere. Kinoe, who until recently had been living in the red-light district, sat sideways on a futon smoking a cigarette. She wore a peach-colored shift, and her neck was powdered white. The house stank of rotten fish.

"I gave up horse trading," answered the brother, counting the cans beside Ueda no Hide.

"Your mother scolded you, you mean. Running around, never settling down to any one thing, " said Hide, who was wearing only underwear.

"You think she can scold me? That stopped when we ran out of money."

"Hah! Money, he says." Ueda no Hide laughed. His eyes narrowed to a slit. Next to him, the man laughed too and then spat again.

"Money's worth shit now. If you're going to buy a woman just take a few pounds of potatoes. Same for cows and horses." Ueda no Hide turned to Kinoe. "Give 'im that half-eaten can."

"But I haven't had any yet," answered Kinoe.

"No matter, no matter, just give him some, there's plenty for you."

The man came into the entranceway and sat down on the step up into the house. Kinoe held out an unlabeled, knife-scarred can to the brother, who was squatting in the flat area just inside the door. "It's sweet," she offered. She smelled faintly of makeup or alcohol. The brother hesitated. Should he take it or not? His mother's words held him back. She had taught him that all prostitutes had V.D. You couldn't let them touch you, and if you touched something that had brushed against their mouths or hands, your body would ooze pus, scabs would form, your nose would fall off, and you'd go crazy.

"What's the matter with you—when I'm offering it to you. It's sweet. You won't get another chance."

"Take it," said the man, handing the can from Kinoe to the brother. "She's givin' it to you."

The brother took the can. Closing his eyes, he swallowed the sweet syrup first. Then plunging his fingers into the can, he took out the moons of fruit and devoured them. The man, Ueda no Hide, and Kinoe burst into laughter.

"If I offered you five of those cans in exchange for your mother, what'd you do?" teased the man.

Kinoe laughed so hard she choked. The man began talking with Ueda no Hide.

"We gotta do it," said the man.

"Now, now." Ueda no Hide wanted to calm him down.

"Who the fuck does he think he is! But you watch me..., I'll show his sorry ass..."

"You've got a one-track mind, Yasu," Hide responded.

"What're you saying? You afraid?" the man snarled.

The brother couldn't understand what they were talking about. He crouched in the earthen entranceway to Ueda no Hide's house and dropped stray pieces of rice straw into the empty can. He had often seen the man get angry. Had seen him in two fights. While the other guy was talking, the man kept silent. But the moment the other guy relaxed his guard, the man struck him in the face or chin with the force of his large frame as if to say you don't fight with words but with the strength that's coiled up inside your body. He never said a thing. The violence inside him just came bursting out.

♌

The son had seen it too. With his own eyes. It made him feel that his own body was directly linked to the man's. Something was stirring inside him. Without a word you knock your opponent down with force. He had a vivid memory. When he was in third grade they were having a sports meet at school. The son had never thought the man would show up. Then he saw the fight near the toilet. The man had knocked another man down and then melted into the crowd as if he felt sheepish and regretted unleashing such violence. The fight's loser had risen groggily. The son's friends were all in a frenzy. "He's incredible!" they were saying, "Let's follow him," even though they were supposed to be having a scavenger hunt. But where had the man gone? The son participated in the scavenger hunt, but as he went around gathering up glasses, a watch, even an old man from the spectators, he could feel the man's eyes singling him out in the crowd.

ʦ

"We gotta do it anyway, Hide. We've come this far. Can't run away now."

"Like I would," Ueda no Hide protested.

The brother's ankles had gone to sleep from crouching in the entranceway, and finally he tumbled backward.

"Whattsa matter with him?" the man grunted. Even now he looked as though he were about to spit through the gap in his teeth. The brother stood up.

"Here, run these cans over to the old man in Iriai, and tell him they're from Ueda no Hide," Kinoe ordered.

The brother hesitated.

"Go," said the man.

ʦ

That night a huge fire started in the red-light district and spread to Tokiwachō and Nakajitō. It was the dead of night. The flames blew up, sparks flying from the red-light district and past the station to the new part of town. Rumor had it that the fire had started in the brothel Yafuku, that somebody with a grudge against Yafuku had set it. Maybe it was one of the whores whose plans to run off with a man fell through and who set the fire in desperation. Or, some said, it was the brother of a woman sold to the brothel who felt so sorry for his sister having to service so many men that he pretended to be a customer, asked for his sister, went up to her room, killed her with his own hands, and then torched the place. At the scene the spectators were saying, "It's a whore fire. No stopping it once it gets going. Just wait till it burns itself out." The wind blew stronger. The flames roared up straight to the sky and slowly fanned outward. Keeping his eyes off the fire, the brother searched out the man and found him staring, mesmerized, at the flames. The man had been completely transformed. His body looked three times larger than his own. He was absolutely terrifying. Where the hell had he come from, and why had he come? Just the sight of him mingling with the crowd, watching the fire nonchalantly, then joining in when the others said it was a whore fire—it terrified him. How could the man watch so impassively? He who had set the fire. But nobody knew anything about him, this man standing in the crowd, arms folded across his chest like some demonic guardian king—where he came from, who his parents were, how he'd spent his time, his birthdate, his age, his true name. The only known fact was that he was a drifter who came from some other place than here. A no-good bum, but from where? It was a riddle. The brother watched the man and the fire burning behind him. Word came from somewhere that the bodies of two prostitutes had been found. The brother told the man. The man snorted through his nose, "Ha, ha, well, it's a whore fire, so they're bound to come up with a few of them." The man pressed his big hand down on the brother's head. Stop talking and watch the fire, the hand seemed to say. At the same time, it communicated the man's ambivalence about this fire, his regret as well as his awe. When the pillars of one house began to crumble, a shout went up from the crowd. Youth Association firemen in happi coats circled around the fire but made no headway. The flames moved to the eaves of the large house next door. "It's Ozeki's place," someone shouted. The big hand rubbed the brother's head briskly. Burn, burn, the hand was saying. Then a voice called out at the back of the crowd, and men in happi coats parted the spectators so they could haul in a hose to renew the fight. The man tapped the brother on the head. The brother followed him. Why had the man set the fire? Did he hold a grudge? Or, as the wild but convincing rumor had it, did he set a murderous fire to avenge a sister sold into prostitution? The next day, his mother came home with some new gossip, and this rumor seemed closer to the mark. Tokiwachō, Uinoji, Nakajitō, and the new part of town all belonged to the Sakura family. Someone who held a grudge against Sakura or his property had set the fire. Several different places had all burned at the same time. "I can't say this too loud, but if it was against the Sakuras, there's no reason to cry about it," said the mother. But the brother laughed. The man was an employee of the hated Sakura. So, said the brother, Sakura must have ordered the man to do it.

❦

The brother went over to Ueda no Hide's house and found the man there drinking. "Ah, there you are," said the man. The brother didn't go in. Spitting like the man, he just stood on the worn earth by the front door. Hide's house was a dump. The door to the neighboring house was wide open, and he could see a woman washing something out back. "We had a good time yesterday," said the man. "What a relief," Kinoe tittered drunkenly and drew up one knee. Outside in the street, four children were playing hopscotch. The man touched the fleshy part of Kinoe's thigh.

"Hey Yasu, I'm no girl for sale you know. I'm Hide's wife."

"No big deal," said Ueda no Hide. He was drunk. "Haven't I always said—better to keep a friend than a wife, trust your friend before your wife."

"That does not please me," intoned Kinoe.

The brother stood in the entranceway.

"Come in, come in," said Ueda no Hide, "One of these days I'm going to buy you some cows and horses. Tell your mother: looks like Ueda no Hide's going to set me up and make me into a dealer yet."

"Big promises as usual," said Kinoe, looking for a response from the brother.

Kinoe rearranged the hem of her kimono and stood up, exhaling loudly. "Little brother, come in, it's our victory party."

Kinoe took the brother by the hand. It was chilly and firm. Again, he could smell makeup and alcohol.

"Let's see. How far back was that now... every time you came to see me, promising you'd ransom me. Liar."

"Shudd-up," said Ueda no Hide.

"How can you tell me to shut up? First you sell your own wife to the brothel, gamble with the money, and then ransom me out when times get better!"

"Wife, wife you say?" answered Hide draining his cup.

"At least I've got something to be thankful for anyway. Even good girls are getting sold to the brothels these days."

The brother sat cross-legged next to the man. The man poured sake into a cup and urged him to drink up. It was a strong-smelling homemade brew. Obeying the man's order— "Down it in one gulp"—the brother drained his cup. "Good job, good job," cheered the man and Hide. Pouring him a second cup, the man asked, "So you had a good time yesterday?"

The brother nodded.

"Stick with me and you'll always have a good time." The man and Ueda no Hide laughed.

The cans that had been piled by the door yesterday were gone now. In their place were four wicker trunks overflowing with red kimonos.

The brother felt drunk. He dozed off. It was just around noon. The voices of children playing outside mingled with those of the man and Ueda no Hide. The brother had never once played like a child. His mother had had her hands full supporting him and his three sisters, and she paid no attention to where he went, who his friends were, or whether he was actually working but making it look like he was just hanging out and fooling around—maybe because she couldn't keep an eye on him anyway or thought he was old enough to take care of himself at age eleven or twelve. His mother went out bartering things. In those days you couldn't get along without goods to trade. But anybody with possessions could survive. Money wasn't enough. Everyone made working and living into a game. They made their suffering into a game, too.

"Poor thing. Falling asleep in such a place," said Kinoe. She pinched the brother's nose shut. He breathed through his mouth.

"Don't tease him. Let him sleep," Ueda no Hide scolded her.

Unsure of how long he had slept, the brother woke to the sound of Kinoe's voice saying, "Look, it's raining." He could hear the rain.

"Yeah, it's rainin' all right," the man echoed.

Suddenly, the brother felt worried. Where would his mother take cover from the rain? Wouldn't his three sisters get wet playing outside again and catch colds? His second sister had come down with pleurisy and was lucky to be alive. She was a shy girl

who often threw up or ran a fever, and she had a morbid fear
of germs. This sister was most like their father, and he in turn
had loved her best. He had to sell property in the mountains and
farmland in order to pay for her doctor. The doctor had told him
that in all probability she wouldn't live. The father would come
back from work and say to her, "You sweet little thing," and then,
quickly changing out of his work clothes, he'd massage the girl,
whose breath was feverish and who could barely move her limbs.

"Sweet little thing, get better, get better and I'll dress you in a
red kimono and put a pin in your hair." When the father touched
the girl's body, she cried out as if to communicate her pain to
him. The little girl had a major operation on her back and survived. But later the father had died.

"Oh, even a little rain cheers me up," said Kinoe. "It makes me
feel alive," she continued laughing. "In the brothel, you know, I
was the only one happy when it rained."

"That's 'cause you're such a slut," said Ueda no Hide.

"Yeah, I guess so. If I hadn't been a slut, you wouldn't have
sold me to the brothel, right? And I wouldn't be waiting for sweet
words from you when all you talk is crap. Right, Yasu? Everybody complains about the rain but I used to say, 'Rain, rain, rain
pouring down from the sky,' and somehow it gave me strength.
If you'd come to see me then, I'd have treated you so well, the
madam would have blown her top!"

"It's comin' down," said the man.

The rain pattered on the zinc roof. Ueda no Hide looked over
at the brother.

"Look, Yasu's little helper has woken up."

The brother sat up. His ears and head felt hot. Outside it was
light. Drops of rain bounced off the street and spattered the paper
in the windows. As the brother yawned, the man poked him in the
head.

"Eat," he ordered, handing him a chicken thigh. The brother stared at it blankly.

"Don't worry, it ain't dog meat," the man laughed.

The man's eyes looked blue. The brother remembered how red they had shone in the glow of the fire the night before. The man's eyes, nose, and mouth were set in a cruel mask. The opposite of his own father's. His father's face had been kind. But the man's face frightened him. And besides, the man was so big.

The son thinks that he looks like the man. What does it mean to know that you look like another human being? In the last twenty years the man's hair has thinned on top. The guys at work have started to tease the son, saying, "It's looking a little thin up there," and whenever he hears this, he jumps. "Maybe you're not getting enough," his friends joke. "How about a trip to the Turkish bath after the last round? It looks bad, a young guy going bald because he isn't getting enough."

"I'm not a young guy going bald, I'm a middle-aged one," the son answers. Yamamoto, who is changing his work clothes by the locker, naked from the waist up, speaks as if letting the secret slip out: "Hey, you're not bald. You were just trimming your hair with a razor in the bath and lopped off a little too much. We know that. But you're so fucked up you even blowdry your pubic hair and give it a side part."

The man drank. He laughed. The hard rain continued. Through the wall of the house next door they could hear a child crying. The brother stared vacantly at the paper window.

The man was eating meat. "Ya want any?" he asked poking the brother on the head again. The brother shook his head. Everything was soaked. The barley fields in front of the house, the ditches, the communal well. He felt anxious but didn't know why. Even sad. His eyes were drawn to the red kimonos in the wicker trunks. The man and Ueda no Hide ate their meat. There was plenty of food in Ueda no Hide's house, and kimonos that his sisters could wear. But his own house was bare. They ate spoiled food and wore old clothes, things that his mother collected through bartering. Kept indoors by the rain, his three sisters would be in the empty house, eating scraps of taro root and sweet potato peels cooked by their mother, singing songs and playing with their dolls.

"What're you thinkin' about, little brother?" Kinoe asked. "You need a hug?"

"No."

The man snorted, "Hah. Watch yourself 'round Kinoe. She's a pro. The best in the district."

"What're you saying?" laughed Kinoe, shifting position and drawing up her knee.

"Yeah, that's why old Hide here rushed back to ransom you after he'd made a little money. The old lady at Yafuku called him a dupe, an idiot, a dog. But you came out way ahead. Even if he borrowed a fortune to ransom you, the place burned down in the end, so nobody's any the wiser."

Ueda no Hide smirked.

The bottle of sake was empty.

The brother left with the man when the rain turned to drizzle. "Where you going?" he asked, but the man didn't answer. First, they climbed the hill and came onto the charred remains of the red-light district.

"Look, what a mess. Where are men going to go for fun now?"

the man declaimed for the benefit of the others who had come to see the ruins.

Smoke rose on all sides. The landscape was completely altered. Without any houses to block the view, you could see all the way to the new part of town. The place stank of ash.

"Wow. There's a lot more space here now," said the brother.

The man flinched. "Idiot," he said, thumping the boy on the head.

Why had the man jumped on him like that? Perhaps the brother had hit the mark. Uinochi, Tokiwachō, and Nakajitō are now at the heart of the shopping area, with the supermarket, bank, department store, and kimono shop all in a row.

Next they went to Old Gon's house in the new part of town. The man had cash. Five men were gambling. The man went inside. With a straw mat over the doorway, the place looked like a shed. Outside, the brother played with the goat, pulling up the grass that grew on the mountainside and feeding it to her. The grass was wet with rain. The goat ate, shaking her sagging teats. After a while, sounds of an argument carried out of the house. The man rushed outside followed by a red-faced man. Both were barefoot. The red-faced man was in his underwear, his arms covered with tattoos. "Fuck you," he shouted, striking out at the man. The blow landed on the man's shoulder. "You and your big fuckin' mouth!" Red-face kicked the man. He missed. The man was silent.

"Whaddaya mean tryin' to make a fool of me? Where do you think you are? You're not even from around here!"

Old Gon poked his head out from behind the matting. "Stop it, stop it, the police'll come."

Red-face punched the man on the nose and he fell back on the grass near the goat shed. The man got up flustered. With his eye on Red-face, he grabbed the pole used to bar the goat pen and swung, aiming at the head, but the pole glanced off Red-face's shoulder. Brushing the pole off, Red-face took a step forward. This time the man whacked him directly in the face with the pole. Blood spurted out. Red-face fell and the man began beating him across the torso.

"Stop, stop!" screamed Old Gon rushing out. The man kept kicking Red-face between the legs. Gon lunged at the man. The other gamblers poured out of the house. "Hey," called the man to the brother and then ran off, his feet still bare. The brother just stood there. The man ran as though his feet had wings.

Before long the man was going in and out of the brother's house. Then he was there all the time. The mother got pregnant. When the mother was six months pregnant with the son, the man was picked up for gambling. If it had only been that, the mother probably wouldn't have broken with him, but at the time the man had two other women and both of them were pregnant, too. It was just like him. The mother hated him for it. Holding her big belly, she went to the local jail to scold him for being such a liar.

By the time the man got out of jail, the son was already three years old. The man made a beeline for the mother's house. She lost her temper. Then he sought out the son. The son couldn't remember exactly, but supposedly he had told the man, "You don't take care of me, you're not my father!" Using these same words, his mother brusquely rejected the man's entreaties and chased him off, telling him not to show his face again.

That same man was now dying. The night before when the son got home from the day shift, a phone call had come from his mother in the country, almost as if she had been anticipating his return. His stepfather spoke first. Then the mother came on. The man was about to die, his mother said tersely. He'd been riding a motorcycle and had crashed into a tree branch, breaking his ribs.

It seemed funny to him somehow.

"Isn't he a bit old to be riding a motorcycle?" he asked.

"You would think so," replied his mother. "Even so, he imagines he's still one of the boys. But it's over for him now, it's over."

Then his mother put the question to him, asking him whether he would come back to see his father die.

"You're grown up now, I won't tell you what to do. You decide on your own."

He answered that he wouldn't go.

All his life he had felt the man's gaze on him. When he was twelve, his brother, then twenty-four years old, had killed himself. Since then he had felt the gaze of the dead on him—assuming his brother's voice, breath, and eyes lived on in the realm of the dead. But the man, he realized, had been watching him with the gaze of the living. Still, everyone dies. Everyone fades away. As he'd said the other night when his mother called him, "They just keep on dying."

"What a shock," his wife said. "I kept asking you to introduce me to him whenever we went out there and now....Now there'll be one less thing to look forward to. You know, your sister takes her youngest out on a stroll around town, but she never asks me to go along. They're his grandchildren, aren't they, and I'm his daughter-in-law."

"They're not his grandchildren; you're not his daughter-in-law."

"Poor man."

"Poor man? He was happy with things the way they were. He watches you from the shadows. If I dumped you and got together with another woman, and then spied on our kids and met them on the sly, you'd better not feel sorry for me. Men like to be that way. A man is happiest when he can make people think he's just some wandering free spirit."

"But then you're never at peace."

"Peace, fuck peace, ain't no such thing." He spat out the words.

On an impulse he made a call to his second oldest sister. He didn't believe his mother.

"He's badly hurt, they're saying he might not make it," his sister told him.

His wife's parents, who lived with them, were watching him from where they sat on the sofa. His four-year-old and nineteen-month-old daughters were playing with wooden blocks. His sister, the only one still left in their hometown, didn't ask if he was coming home.

"Really? So it's true then," he said hanging up the phone.

He sat down next to his children. The children ignored him, building a house and a tower out of triangles, squares, and circles before knocking it down. Their own house was tiny, but actually not so small for a pre-fab. Downstairs was a six-mat room and an eight-mat room that served as a living room/dining room, and upstairs they had a four-and-a-half-mat and a six-mat room. It was definitely bigger than the house they had been renting up until last year. That rental had been on a farm, and he'd gotten into too many fights with the owners in the main house. The farmer's insensitivity infuriated him. After the night shift, he'd be dozing and the farmer would rev up his tilling machine even though the land there was the size of a postage stamp. The children would be making noise, too. Finally, he'd dash out in bare feet in his underwear and confront the farmer, yelling "Hey, asshole, what the hell are you doing, making a racket all day long. How'd you like me to smash that fucking toy of yours!"

The landlady would then rush out saying, "Easy, take it easy!"

They decided to split a loan with his wife's parents, who were also living in a rental, and leave the cramped, uninhabitable house for this one.

His wife's parents were at a loss for words. "That man he's talking about, he's your son-in-law's secret love," the woman explained to her parents.

"You idiot, you're talking nonsense," the son interjected.

"Hadn't you better go?" asked his mother-in-law.

"Why bother. Why should I go see him die?"

"Mmm," murmured his mother-in-law, falling silent.

"You know, I've been thinking about getting a piano," said his father-in-law, changing the subject. His father-in-law was a piano tuner.

"A piano, you mean, a real piano?"

"There's a cheap piano for sale at Uchiyama's place. I'd tune it properly and repair it."

"A Steinway?" teased the woman. "If you get just any old piano, you're just going to feel embarrassed when people come over."

"I'm not about to bring just any old piano into the house," laughed the father. "Even if it's not a Steinway, there are still good pianos."

Absentmindedly the son sat down next to his two daughters and watched them play with the wooden blocks. They were just out of the bath, so they were in their nightgowns. He hugged his youngest daughter from behind but she threw him off with a whine. Suddenly he felt tears welling up. What was that man to him? He had inherited his big body—and no doubt his temper, too. Now they were saying that the man had gone and crashed his motor-cycle into a tree like some stupid kid.

He wanted everything washed clean. Made pure. During his next night shift, he couldn't stop thinking about the man and his older brother, the one who had first introduced the man to his mother. It was raining and the wind was blowing. The cold rain pricked his skin.

"Hey, Mr. Two-thousand Pounds." The American named Willie joked around like he always did.

"Idiot, what're you talking about, you hairy ape? It's Mr. Three-thousand Pounds to you," he answered.

During his three-hour sleep break, he went to the bath.

"Aren't you going to blowdry your pubic hair today?" someone teased.

"It gets all mussed up anyway when I go to bed," he answered. Soon after he left for the club. There was a jukebox. He listened to the same Harumi Miyako record over and over again.

"Guess he likes it," said one of his friends.

✥

He was drunk. On the third go-round they'd gone to a cabaret. He had spent all his money and then taken a cab home. After that he had gone wild, and for no good reason at all. He hit the woman. Kicked her. Smashed the glass chandelier with a dining-room chair. Dumped over the double-door refrigerator with the same brute strength the American had teased him about. He'd been in an unbelievably good mood with his friends. But when he saw his wife's sleepy, irritated expression looking back at him as she paid the driver his fare, he lost his temper.

"What're you saying, that I'm just a bum?"

He shoved his dazed wife into the entranceway, dragged her by her hair into the living room, slammed the door, and immediately started in hitting her.

"What's wrong with being a bum, huh?"

Absorbing the full force of the blows, the woman fell back on her buttocks and struck the wall by the phone where her father had said he would put the piano.

"Just tell me what's wrong with it!" he yelled at her. Fire was coursing through his body. He stared at her.

Huddling against the wall, the woman kept her eyes cast downward. She didn't try to reason with him or make a move...maybe sensing this was the best way to deal with him.

Still, he didn't like her attitude.

"Get up," he said.

When she didn't respond, he kicked her. She crouched next to the wall, shielding her head with her hands, curled up on herself.

Usually the woman had a lot to say. Before he got his present job—when he was unemployed—she had sent him off to a number of places. He had one interview after another and was turned down everywhere. Finally he got a job through a high school friend. The woman had told him to go here and there, and, steeling himself, he had gone to those interviews for the sake of the family. But she had never experienced the shame he felt when they rejected him with "I'm sorry, but you're not the right person for the job." They were right of course; he wasn't the right person for the job. And he never would be. With his rough hands he wasn't the right person to be taking out pearls for elegant women customers at his wife's cousin's accessories store, or to say to them seductively, "This would look wonderful on you." His wife was obviously ten times better equipped to deal with the real world than he was. But now...she was quiet. Wearing dowdy yellow pajamas under a robe that looked more like a nurse's gown, she cowered, her rear end sticking up in his direction.

"You shit," he said, giving her a judo kick in the ass that slammed her head into the wall.

"Now tell me. What you said before about being a bum."

"You're the one who said it," the woman answered tearfully,

placing her hands on the floor. Her head was still pressed to the wall. "I never said anything like that. I was just nodding my head when you said it."

"Liar." He grabbed the collar of her robe. The woman by now was exhausted, and when he yanked she fell over. Her forehead began to swell up. He examined her face, saw her frightened eyes watching him, and then kicked her again without saying a word. The woman didn't cry or scream.

Her parents rushed in.

"What's going on?" asked her father, blinking.

"Stay out of it. Stay out. This is between a man and his wife. Don't come in here—it's our problem," he said, pushing his father-in-law out of the room and closing the door.

The woman didn't cry. He took the whiskey from the bookshelf next to the sofa and poured some out into a teacup that was sitting there too. The woman, her parents, and the children must have been drinking tea late into the evening. He swallowed the whiskey in one gulp.

"So?" he said to her, "you think of me that way? Shit. That's just great."

She looked up. She sensed he had calmed down.

"You're the one who said that about your father."

"My father? Who are you talking about?"

She was silent. Then suddenly she started to cry.

"Stop crying," he thundered.

"There's no reason for me to say that. You know better than anyone."

"I'm a bum, he's a bum," he replied. "Listen, let me repeat myself, if you keep calling that asshole 'father' like we're one big happy family, I'm going to break your fuckin' neck. He's not my father, he's a bum, the biggest deadbeat there ever was." Suddenly the sadness hit him. He didn't know why. Everyone dies, he thought. Everyone disappears. Nobody will be left in this world, the world of the living. He couldn't stand the thought, and instinctively kicked at the sofa with his feet. Suddenly he was mauling the cushions that his wife's parents had used since their days in the rental house.

"Stop it," his wife said.

"Shut up!" he yelled.

Then he lurched over to pick up the double-door refrigerator they had just bought and heave it outside. Like the strongman Kintoki lifting up a bear in his daughters' storybook, he started to wrestle with it. Milk containers and assorted colored Tupperware filled with his mother-in-law's leftovers came crashing down off the shelves. He could hoist the refrigerator up, but he couldn't quite lift it high enough. It weighed a thousand pounds empty but was even heavier now because it was filled with pieces of half-eaten cheese, leftover pickles, lettuce, and cucumbers, and half-grapefruits. Bracing himself like a sumo wrestler tipping over his opponent, he hurled the refrigerator sideways. Next he went to smash the color television. He couldn't stand television. In the farmer's house he wouldn't let his wife and daughters watch even a black and white TV. It just bothered him too much. It was especially irritating when he came off the night shift. He'd wake up in the evening, and his wife would have the television on low and be stifling her laughter. Now he'd smash their new color TV. But then he imagined his daughters wailing over the broken TV when they woke up in the morning. He hesitated. Instead he grabbed a dining room chair, brandished it over his head, and smashed the mini-chandelier. The fixture—which had been featured in the realtor's ads and photos of the house—was the latest household accessory of the day. The lights went out and the glass shattered. He swiped one last time at the chandelier and then put the chair down.

In the morning he awoke in the room upstairs. The house was strangely quiet. His wife was lying on her stomach with her arm around their younger daughter, asleep in the daughters' four-and-a-half-mat room. The older daughter was gone. He went downstairs. His wife's parents were gone too. The chandelier had been removed from its socket. Things didn't look much different from usual. In fact the place was tidier than usual. Everything was clean. Empty. What had happened, he wondered.

"Hey, what happened to your mother and Noni, where are they?" he yelled up at the sleeping woman. He heard the rustle of the younger child waking up. Then the voice of his wife scolding the child, "Don't pay any attention."

The woman didn't answer. He took a piss. It stank of alcohol. He realized he was hungry. He climbed to the second floor to tell the woman to make him something to eat right away. His daughter who had just woken up looked at him and called, "Papa, Papa," beaming as if she hadn't seen him for a year. His wife stayed on her stomach.

"Hey," he said.

"Papa, Papa," said his daughter, excited now and thrashing under the covers.

"He's not your papa," her mother told her.

"Come here," he said. The child squirmed.

"He's not your papa."

The child, making baby noises, struggled to get up but the woman seemed to be holding her down.

A bird had come to the feeder on the metal fence that separated their house from the one next door. It swallowed whole chunks of stale bread. There seemed to be another bird in the plum tree. The plum had begun to go yellow and wither in midsummer and was now almost bare. The sight hurt his eyes. Outside everything looked transparent. Quiet. He wasn't hung over. It was just how he was: no matter how insanely he drank or how wild he got, physically he never got a headache, felt nauseous, or ran a fever. According to his friends at work and his drinking buddies, it was only his huge body that drank, exulted, then burst into flames. He and his big body were separate, they said. He leaned back on the couch. He felt his heart leap up out of his body and wriggle, twitching as it hit the air, just like the heart of a frog he had dissected in biology class as a boy. The silence was complete. He was standing on the membrane between life and death. His eyes pained him. The bird flew up and away.

The palm of his right hand was red and swollen. Another bird landed on the feeder. It too ate the crumbs of bread. The sun must have moved between the buildings because the area around the feeder was now bathed in light. The sage flowers that grew around the roots of the plum swayed on their stems. Blood red. Some had wilted, their color faded. I want to die just like that, he thought. The way plants wilt and die. In the time he had remained there quiet, the bird had almost polished off the bread crumbs before hopping nimbly along the fence and flying up onto the roof next door. He stared at the rustling sage flowers. "A useless life, so die," he said to himself. "Everybody else lives quietly, everybody suffers in silence, but not you, right?" he addressed the sage flowers. He could see the face of his older brother. These days he often dreamed about him. The brother in his dreams was always bleeding. "Where have you been? I've been looking for you for a long time," he said to the brother.

Suddenly he could see the brother as a child again. He could see the man. It was easy for him, because he had heard the stories about them over and over again from his three sisters, his mother, and his stepfather. Images of his brother and the man rose up vividly. There was a scent of grass. Mugwort. His mother had filled a large basket with fresh mugwort leaves. When was it? She had been very pregnant. And from the time the man had come to live with them their lives had improved dramatically. It was like night and day, now compared with the time his mother had had to go out and barter things around town. It must have been around March 3rd, Girl's Day. The mother had made sweets out of mugwort and flour. The man was lying on his back and lifting the youngest sister up on his feet as he cawed aloud.

"Look, you're a little bird, a kite" he says, supporting her middle on the bottom of his feet and letting go of her hands. Hesitantly the girl stretches out her legs and arms wide like a bird. "Kii, kii, kii," says the man moving his feet. Tickled, the sister laughs.

"O.K. time's up, Shiiyo, you're next." The man beckons to the middle sister, who sits stiffly while her sister tries to make her smile.

"No, no! Me, me," the younger sister shakes herself and races to climb back up on the feet of the man, who is still lying back.

"No good, no good, you have to take turns," answers the man. But his invitation has made the middle sister cautious. She isn't strong. And she dislikes the man. Feels no love for him. The middle sister moves closer to the brother and hesitates, not knowing how to respond to the man's invitation.

"I'm going to do it again, Kii, kii, who's next, who wants me to do it?" says the man. The youngest sister yells, "Me, me" and crawls atop him. His feet supporting her stomach, he holds her hands saying, "Look, how high, kii, kii," and then extends his legs. The youngest sister laughs. Balancing on the man's feet, she chortles. Still laughing, she slips off and lands on her bottom. Without missing a beat, the man solicits, "Who's next?" The youngest sister picks herself up and rushes over to the man saying, "Me!" just as the middle sister runs to his side saying, "Me!"

"Take turns, take turns," the man says, gathering the hands of the middle sister and moving her stomach onto his feet. Just then the sister begins to sniffle, but the man positions her on his feet anyway and raises her up, saying, "Look how high!" She squirms and starts to cry softly. "High in the air, kii, kii," exclaims the man. Now the middle sister is sobbing. She thrashes and falls backward.

"What're you doing?" the mother scolds the man. "She's weak, not like the others, you'll hurt her playing so rough." The man gets up. The middle sister retreats to her brother's side. The brother looks remorseful, as though he's the one being scolded for his sister's crying.

ॐ

The oldest sister resembled the man. Soon she was calling him "Daddy." The youngest sister called him that too. But, despite their mother's instructions, the brother who had first brought the man to his mother and the very shy middle sister wouldn't use the name "Daddy." The brother called the man "Uncle." But even that felt unnatural, so he tried not to call him anything. The middle sister continued to run high fevers, even after the man came on the scene. Her temperature would soar in the middle of the night, and on nights when the man was out gambling, the mother, her belly huge, would rummage for money and then head to the hospital by the station, making the brother carry the sister piggyback. When she didn't have the money, she'd order the brother to bring the man back from the gambling house. If he says he can't stop gambling, just have him give you the money, she'd say. The brother would zoom off. When the man wasn't in the gambling hall, the brother would ask his whereabouts and even go as far as the brothels in the red-light district. There were times when he'd find the man in bed with a prostitute.

The man was kind to the woman and her children. When was it? The son had been in third or fourth grade. His mother had taken him to live with the person who later became his stepfather. It was summer. In those days there were still logs lashed together floating in the river. He and his friends were swimming and playing a game between the logs, throwing in a white stone and then diving for it. The remains of a castle stood overlooking the river. Cicadas were crying. Somebody was watching—the son sensed it somehow. But soon he forgot and became absorbed in the game with his friends. Hour after hour they stayed in the water till their lips turned purple. Then shaking with cold they climbed back up on the logs and threw themselves into the river again.

As he was putting on his clothes and getting ready to leave, he saw the man standing there in the shade of a chinaberry tree. "Hey, boy," the man said. The son felt strangely embarrassed that the man was there and had been watching him all this time. The man spoke in an oddly gentle voice that didn't match his face or his body. No, it wasn't a gentle voice, but a voice made for business deals. The man hadn't abandoned his child. The child had abandoned his father. So of course the man would speak to him like this.

ℭ

The house that belonged to the mother and her children was spacious. Sometimes the grandmother and the uncle from Koza came to stay on. The man would go out horse trading with the uncle. When the uncle discovered that the mother was pregnant, he was overjoyed, almost as if he was expecting his own child. "Really now, really now, good job, good job," he exclaimed. The uncle drank. He got happy and danced. The man just stared at him in wonder.

Hoping to purchase a cow, the man and the uncle went to the mountains and took the brother along. The brother was so happy he felt like he was floating on air. They went to Takamori but didn't find a good animal. Instead they spent most of their money on potatoes, persimmons, and rice, which they stuffed in a sack and carried back. On the way home, they stashed their goods in an air raid shelter to avoid the eyes of the police. As they'd guessed, the police were on the lookout for black marketers. One after another they were confiscating the bags and baskets carried by men and women alike.

It was right then that it happened. The man ran out of luck.

The man and the uncle stopped in at the Yatsuhashi cock-fighting ring. They were planning to go and retrieve the goods in the air raid shelter later. Another uncle, this one from the brother's paternal side, happened to arrive at Yatsuhashi with his son, Kinji. Seeing the brother, Kinji spoke to him.

"Hey, where you been?"

"Nowhere," answered the brother.

The man and the uncle went around the back of the building. "Stay around here," the man ordered. Yatsuhashi's looked like a wealthy farmer's place and had a large house and garden. Kinji was holding two yellow chicks that his father had probably bought for him. Pointing at the well in the garden he said, "That's where they sell 'em." A woman with a kerchief around her head sat on a wooden stool with a box in front of her. Nestled in Kinji's palms, the chicks' eyes remained closed, as if in a trance. But when he touched their heads, they opened their eyes and started pecking.

"This one's nearly dead."

Kinji's laugh exposed his chipped front tooth. He put the other chick down on the ground. It still had some life in it and, looking around, it began to walk. "Make them race," said the brother.

Kinji put the nearly dead one on the ground, too. It staggered along and then came to a halt. The chick closed its eyes. It was trembling as if its head was too heavy for its body. Kinji squatted down and poked the chick's behind. It moved forward again.

The brother suddenly had an idea. "Maybe it would perk up if you gave it some water."

Kinji didn't respond. Perhaps annoyed by the brother's advice, he stuck the chicks back into his pockets. On the other side of the Yatsuhashi well was a stable with a large black horse. For a while the two boys stared at the horse. The brother thought that he might like to become a horse trader. Then the woman from the main house came out and chased them away, "You don't want to get kicked by the horse, so go over there and play by the cocks."

The boys browsed around the cow shed and the shed piled high with kindling and then watched the woman as she burned some straw and twigs, her hands webbed like the feet of a duck, either from a burn or maybe the bomb. It wasn't cold, but they stretched their hands out to the flames anyway. "Oh no," said Kinji. In a panic he took the chicks out of his pockets. Both were dead. "Shit," said Kinji biting his lip. "O.K. now we do this," and he began plucking one of the chicks. He handed the other chick to the brother and told him to do the same. The feathers were tough. Kinji snapped off two bamboo sticks from behind the house. Then he pried open the chick's mouth with the stick, drove it through the body, and held it out to the flames. The chick burned, its feathers crackling. Soon it was black. The brother did the same. "It stinks," said the woman who stirred the fire, scolding them about the smell of the feathers.

As they ripped off the burnt chick's flesh with their teeth, the boys wandered round to the back of the house. About twenty adults were standing there. In a circle of stakes covered in straw matting, two cocks were engaged in a bloody fight. The brother looked for the man and the uncle. The man had left the uncle and was standing next to a man with whiskers peering into the straw circle. The man kept calling, "Watch out, watch out, go round to the right, go, go!" The brother pushed his way in next to the man. Whiskers looked at him. "O.K., O.K.," said Whiskers. The two cocks were smeared in blood. The brown one fastened its beak around the throat of the green one and kicked. Feathers went flying. It looked as if the man had bet on the green cock.

"What're you doing? I'm gonna wring your neck and eat you alive!" a voice cried from the other side. They laughed. The brother was rooting for the man's bird. The two cocks glared at each other. From either side they came pecking at each other's throats and at the flesh below the eyes, their throats locking, flying and clawing at each other with raised talons. Each time they attacked, old feathers stuck in the ring's straw matting danced in the wind they raised.

"Go get him, tear him to pieces!" said the brother.

"The other one's a weakling, a crybaby," said the man putting his hand on the brother's head. The green cock seized the other cock by the eye. "Go," urged the man. Almost instantly the green cock rose up and kicked the other. But then the birds glared at each other again, pecking each other on the neck and kicking. Voices called, "What's the matter? Scared or somethin'?" "Better do it before the sun goes down." Finally one bird pecked the other directly in the eye. It happened in an instant. The brown bird seemed to realize it had scored a direct hit because it began fluttering and kicking with renewed energy. The crowd stirred. The green bird had lost its right eye. Blood was gushing down. In the midst of its blind downfall, the green bird rose up kicking in a last desperate attempt. But it had lost the will to fight and in seconds was being kicked senseless by the brown bird. "It's no good, I lost big," said the man, taking his hand from the boy's head. The green cock had lost both eyes and was staggering about. Someone, probably its owner, stretched out his hands and picked up the bird.

"I'll break your neck, you fuckin' bird," somebody said.

The uncle appeared. Looking into the man's face, he said, "It's too bad, you lost a lot."

"Boy, you want something to eat?" The man took money out of his pocket. "We won't be able to buy a cow or anything with this," he said angrily. "O.K., one more. Let's go for double or nothing."

The man and the uncle drank while the boy ate a sweet made of potato. The uncle looked like his mother. No, they both resembled the grandmother, the result of having had different fathers. He had three uncles in Koza, but none came close in size to the man. When the uncle stood up, he only came up to the man's shoulder.

A man wearing boots passed in front of them holding a black cock with a razor blade lashed to its claw. He put the cock in the straw enclosure. "They shouldn't do that," said the uncle. He sipped the sake in his cup. "You can't tell which one's really the stronger."

"That makes it more fun," said the man standing up. He downed his sake. Looking at the boy he laughed, "Ah, how's this? We'll get it all back and go buy us a cow tomorrow. Forget Takamori, we'll go to Koshiyama instead." The man reeked of sake. "Hey boy, if you get a cow what'll you do with it anyway? Hitch it to a wagon, load up your mother and sisters and a cooking pot and cross the mountains to Tennōji?"

The brother didn't really understand what the man was saying. The name Tennōji was new to him. Where could it be? The man looked at the brother and laughed. At that moment especially, the man seemed to tower over the brother. Who were the man's parents? Where and how had he grown up? The brother didn't have a clue. With a nudge to the head, the man urged him forward.

The man pressed into the crowd around the straw enclosure. Money had been placed on both birds. The man in boots,
who seemed to be in charge of the cockfighting ring, waved a
paper over his head. "Place your bets," he called out as he went
around collecting money. The man bet all the money he had
on him. Soon the cockfight started. The razors tied to their
right legs caused both cocks to move with a slight limp. Each
seemed to take out its discomfort on the other. As they pecked
and kicked each other, the razors dug deep into their flesh,
instantly drenching them in blood. In the shower of blood they
fought even more ferociously. One bird had half its comb dan-
gling down. The other had blood spewing over its black feathers from a deep cut below its eye. Blood spattered the straw
enclosure. The cock with the torn comb was the stronger. It
seized the other by the beak, and with great aplomb dug its talons in deep and ripped. The other let out a scream. It was the
decisive moment, although no one in the crowd quite realized
it. Dripping blood, Screamer limped over to the straw matting
and stood still. Then without warning, the two cocks attacked
each other again. Now the one with the torn comb rolled to the
ground. It got up again. It kicked. But then it collapsed again,
its leg torn open by the razor. Covered in blood Screamer stood
still. For a moment, it seemed to be reflecting, humanlike, on
what it had done. Again, the two birds flew at each other kicking. Comb fell down. Screamer aimed at its eyes and attacked.
It tore at the bird's flesh and clawed with its talons. Comb
couldn't get up. Screamer paused again and lifted its head, perhaps in a show of remorse. Blood poured from a wound above
its beak. "Shit, now what," said the man. Again Screamer
kicked. Then it stood still. "Time's up, time's up," shouted the
man in the boots, but this time he did not pick up his own bird.
The crowd stirred. Left there in the ring, Screamer went on the

attack again as if it couldn't help itself. The man had placed all his money on Comb.

"Let's go, boy" said the man. The brother could feel the man's disappointment.

"But that one squawked first," protested the brother. The man didn't answer.

"Hup to, hup to, or you'll get in trouble with your mother for going to the cockfights again," the man said to the brother. "I'm flat broke."

The man made to leave.

"I guess we can't buy a cow now," said the brother.

The man looked into the brother's face.

"What? If it's money for a cow, we'll get it somehow. If not, then we take the necessary steps. It's simple. You get it?"

"I get it," the brother answered.

The man laughed. The uncle was watching them.

That night the man left the house.

A fire broke out. "Let's go see it!" clamored the older sister, who then got a spanking from her mother. But the older sister didn't cry; the middle sister did, as if it had been her back and buttocks that felt the sting of their determined mother's hand. She seemed to be in real pain. The grandmother held her. She couldn't stop crying. The uncle, his breath smelling of alcohol, comforted her too, saying, "It's all right, it's all right," but she wouldn't stop.

The mother exploded, "What's the matter with that child—I didn't even hit her!" Her awkward girth made her breath labored as she tried to wrest the child from the grandmother. "You keep this up, the mountain witch'll get you!" The middle sister sobbed.

"Shiiyo, come here with me," said the brother. Still crying, the sister crawled into the brother's futon. The youngest sister was already sound asleep. The middle sister burrowed down into the futon as if the sting in her back and buttocks was finally fading.

"Shiiyo, no, you come in bed with me," said the mother. The sister obeyed meekly.

"Me, too," said the eldest sister.

"See what it's like?" the mother addressed the grandmother, who was sitting forlornly with the uncle to keep him company while he drank. "Even though she's all grown up."

"She's still a big baby," laughed the grandmother as she watched the elder sister dive under the covers.

The brother got up from his futon. The mother rebuked him, but the brother ignored her and left the house.

It was the cockfighting ring at Yatsuhashi. The main house was just catching fire. The flames were red, and as he watched they began to turn to gold. The man was there.

"Hey, boy, it's burning, it's burning, a punishment from the cocks," he said, catching sight of the brother. "Ah, no matter how many times I see one, I never get tired of watching a good fire. Look how things fall. Fuckin' yeah!" The man whispered into his ear. "Burn everything to the fuckin' ground!"

As if in response to the man's words, flames surged up in the middle of the main house.

"It's burning, it's burning," said the brother.

What had the brother felt watching the fire? The man had set it, that was certain. Just as with Ueda no Hide and the brother's help he had set fires all over the red-light district. It was the man's work. Sparks exploded from the flames. The firemen doused the fire with water, but nothing did any good. "Out of the way, get out of the way!" a voice yelled and the crowd parted. The horse was being led out. It bucked and almost snapped its reins. The muscles of its black body rippled. Flames crawled over the roof.

Fanned by the wind, they twisted and towered up, then suddenly evaporated. But soon they crept back up again.

"Fascinating. Fire burns and disappears, and there's no trace," said the man. Mountains rose up behind the Yatsuhashi house. Next to it, other houses with bark-shingled roofs had been crammed together at the foot of the slopes. Each time a spark leapt toward the houses, the crowd stirred. Men poured water on the bark roofs and the wooden walls. Steam could be seen rising in the light of the flames.

"Hey, no matter how big a house is, it's still made of wood and paper, eh, boy?" said the man. "And when they burn they crackle!" The brother looked at the man's face. "The horse got loose!" yelled somebody from the Yatsuhashi house who was standing behind the throng of spectators. The crowd rumbled. Then, as if all reason had returned, the man leaned over and whispered in the brother's ear, "Hey, boy, go home to your mother."

"Why?" the brother grumbled.

"Why, you say? Because you'll get in trouble with your mother again for going off with me. Go home, be on the watch for fire, and sleep. When you wake up in the morning, there'll be a red calf right in front of you. Just like magic."

The brother frowned. The flames rose again. Both their faces glowed.

⅌

Sage flowers trembled in the wind. They bent forward as if bowing, then straightened again. Next to them was a polyanthus plant that the woman had bought that spring from a nursery and transplanted into the garden after its flowers had faded. The plant had waxy leaves and resembled *gishigishi*, a grass they plucked on hillsides and vacant lots to feed to the goats. Now the sage flowers bent down so low they seemed to be attached to the polyanthus. The sight of those flowers shuddering in the wind pained him. Flowers and grass are straightforward. They exist. I'm inferior to the grass, the son whispered to himself as he went to the sink. He drank some water. When he'd been out drinking, he seemed to have completely forgotten about the man. So what had reminded him the instant he got back home? Did it mean he recognized the man as another father in addition to the father he already had? No, that was impossible. The ones who claimed me as a child were my mother, brother, three sisters, uncle, and stepfather. When I graduated from middle school, my stepfather put me down as his child in the family register. So what's that man to me? My biological father? Only in his wildest dreams. The thought makes me laugh. Still, that man gave me life. Actually he only gave the sperm my mother needed to get pregnant with me. That's the truth. But what's the truth mean? I've never lived with that man, never been hugged by him, never felt him rub my head—only been watched by him from a distance. My mother put a stop to all that. I, my mother's child, put a stop to all that. When he got out of prison, he came right away to my mother's door. I'll go straight, we'll give it one more try, he vowed, but she turned him away. At least give me the child—he's my first and besides, he's a boy. Then I did what my mother had taught me to do and said, "You don't take care of me, you're not my father!" The man left, finally. It would have been fine if I'd been a baby monkey or a puppy. Or the child of some native who idles his days away eating potatoes and picking bananas from trees heavy with fruit…. Suddenly, his own thoughts amused him. For all he knew, he was that native. No matter how he looked at it, nothing was going to change the fact that the man was real and so was his stepfather. And the method the man chose to die—hopping on a motorcycle and slamming into the branch of a tree—

suited him perfectly. For his part, the man was expecting his one daughter and two sons to uphold the legitimate relationship of father and child, where both sides recognize the other. But at the same time, even though what existed between them could not be named, had the man intended that another son, with the same face and body as his own, would be here now waiting for him to breathe his last as if it were as natural as grass withering? No, maybe he hadn't intended that after all. Even now the man might be eagerly awaiting his son's arrival... for the reunion of a parent and child whose relationship had been kept a secret, like in old dramas and stories. Seeing the man bandaged around the head and chest, the son would suddenly feel a rush of longing and affection, and his blood would pound through his veins, because after all they were fellow human beings, not dogs, or monkeys, or beasts, and he would call to the man with the raspy breath, "Father!" His eyes brimmed over with tears. He caught his breath. How many times had he thought, "I want to see you and go live with you." Every day as a child he had thought how good it would be if they could live together calling each other "father" and "son" without restraint. Maybe they had plenty of reasons to be mad at each other. But when he told the man they were not father and son, what if the man had just said, "What? But you're only three years old!" Instead, it was as if the man had been holding him to those words of a three year old all this time. Ah, the man who brought me into the world is dying. Father. My father, my true father. It makes me weep. My tears stream down. Must you die already? Do you go to the other world? My brother hanged himself at twenty-four, and I was only twelve. My grandmother died. My uncle too. One by one everyone I love has died. Now, must you go too?

The son stood up. He pushed open the door. Its paint showed recent scratches from a sharp object. First he drank some water in the bathroom. Then he took a piss. Little footsteps sounded on the stairs. His youngest daughter appeared in her best clothes holding her quilt and pillow in either hand. Without these two things, his daughter wouldn't go to sleep no matter what they did. She stared at him as he sat on the couch. "Papa, Papa," she ran to him laughing.

"Chako—," called her mother as she lay in the second-floor bedroom. But the daughter curled herself around his knees calling, "Papa, Papa," as if she hadn't heard. He picked her up. He stroked her thin frizzy hair. Before long she pushed his hand away saying, "No, no." She stepped down onto the bathroom floor. Stamping her feet, she ran over to the sink, and then just as she had seen her mother and grandmother do, she banged on the stainless silver tap demanding, "Water, water." He stood up, walked over to the sink, and poured water into a cup with a girl's face on it. The daughter pushed away the cup saying, "No, no." The water spilled. More vehemently, she said, "Water, water." This time he filled a cup that had a picture of a baby deer. She took it without a fuss.

She had him read her a book. Over and over they looked at the picture of a dove soaring through the sky and below it the character named Moomin waving good-bye. "Flap, flap, coo, coo," he imitated the sound of the dove's wings and its cry. He cuddled his daughter and stroked her head. His hand was so big that her head fit inside his palm. The sky was blue. The white dove was looking down sadly on the small figure of Moomin in the grass. "Good-bye Moomin. Good-bye dove. Someday we'll meet again," he read, feeling as if the words of the book were being whispered in his ear. He could hear the flapping of the dove's wings as it called, coo, coo. Where do you think you are going? he asked the bright white dove. Are you coming here to us in Tokyo?

He looked at his daughter. Last night was like a bad dream.

Help me, he thought. And if you can, save them from what I see with my own eyes. I want to be a gentle, quiet man. Not a murderer or the victim of murder. I don't want to beat anyone up or get beaten up. I want to be a kind person. A good person. He cradled his daughter in his arms. When he tickled her stomach, she laughed. His daughter's stomach pushed back swollen and hard as if something were stuffed inside it.

His wife came downstairs. Her face was swollen, and there was a reddish-black bruise on her cheek. She went into the bathroom. Minutes passed. When she came out, she announced, "I want a separation."

She sat down.

"Father and Mother are old and it's hell for them to see their daughter beaten half to death. You get drunk and you don't know what you're doing. But we're not drunk. When you go crazy, no one can stop you. I remember one time you were out with your friends, and you went crazy. You probably don't even remember it, but you threw off the guy who tried to stop you and then went to kill him. You're a demon when you drink. The rest of the time you have a short fuse, but you're kind. Mother and Father worried about that when we bought this house. . . ."

"It's because I heard that guy was dying."

"That guy? What kind of nonsense is that? It has nothing to do with me, I don't want to hear about it. You don't remember what you did last night? Father and Mother got up in the morning and tidied everything up. Cleaned it all away. The chairs were broken, the refrigerator on its side, pieces of the chandelier scattered everywhere. Try and imagine how my parents feel."

She burst into tears.

"It's hell. You make hell around you."

"If that's the case, I'll give you a separation," he said. "But just one thing, when the time comes, I'll kill you, your parents, and the kids," he said stroking his daughter's head as she sat with the book open on her lap. "I'm not joking. If everything's gonna fall apart, at least I'll do that. I'm not goin' with my tail between my fuckin' legs."

The woman stopped crying. She stared at him.

"How could you do something like that without a reason?" she asked.

"A reason? I'll just make one up afterward," he replied, "It's six of one, half a dozen of another."

"Fine, go ahead. If you're going to kill us, do it, if that will satisfy you."

"Yeah, I'll smash open your head with an ax. I'm not some helpless asshole who stands around wringing his hands."

"Oh, you mean like my father." The woman tensed. "You're not one to judge him."

"Fuck it. If I say I'm going to do something, I do it. You think too much. That's why I hit you." He put his daughter off his knee. She protested. He picked her up again and stroked her head.

"Only a scum hits a woman." His wife lowered her voice. "I'm sick of it. Whenever you drink, you do horrible things. I'm lying there crying, holding onto the children because I'm in pain and I can't sleep, and you're spread-eagled, drunk out of your mind, snoring in your sleep. And you sleep like the dead. God, how many times have I wanted to stab you with a kitchen knife. What exactly am I to you? A punching bag for you to practice on? An animal for you to kick around? What am I to you? I don't know what happened last night with your friends but the minute you get home you start punching and kicking me. Do you even remember what set you off?" the woman asked.

He shook his head.

"You don't even remember. Something you don't even remember was your excuse to go crazy. At first it was because you said I had called your father a bum. But then it was because I wouldn't agree with you when you said he was a bum."

"That guy," he said staring at her, "he's not my father."

"It's a mess. What you say and what you do. I've had enough, I'm tired. I have a life. My mother and father have a life. The world doesn't revolve around you—we live in worlds of our own, my father and I. The children are growing up. Noni already knows. She knew what it meant when mother said we were going to Murakawa. She brought her clothes and told Mother to get her dressed. Usually she cries and struggles, but this time she cooperated."

"Little traitor," he said in a small voice.

"She knows all about it. That her father went crazy again, pushed over the refrigerator, smashed the chandelier. I can't take it anymore. I'm exhausted."

"Well, well," he teased. "You'd better break up with that awful guy right away. Break up with him and get together with me."

"I'm exhausted. You're not a bad person, I know that, it's all this stuff you keep inside, when you drink too much it all comes out. You think people are insects, don't you, and you're the only human being in the world, but tell me, what is the difference between you and me? Just try and tell me. Give me one reason why a man should beat up a woman."

"That other guy is the bad one. He's got too much fuckin' energy wound up inside. It's a crime to let a man like that drink."

"If you know that, don't drink! Why drink till you go crazy?" The woman stood up. She tried to snatch the daughter from his lap. The daughter resisted. He held the daughter between his knees.

"Think of Mother and Father. When I was growing up Father never even tapped me on the head, and now he sees his own daughter being beaten up right in front of him. My parents are just trying to lead a happy life with their grandchildren, and you destroy the house. It was fine for them to split the repayment of the loan and the money we borrowed for a deposit, but look at if from their point of view. This is the house where they can take it easy in their old age, and then a demon comes along and destroys it. You aren't even human."

"A no-good jerk-off bum."

"You are a demon without blood or tears, wearing human skin. But we're not demons, we're human."

"Say whatever the fuck you want."

He ached. A tingling pain emanated from somewhere in his body. Was the man dead already, he wondered. Head cracked. Face crushed. In a free fall, his chest slammed to the ground, his ribs snapping. Bones protruding from the skin. Bones piercing his organs. Heart lanced. But still alive in spite of it all. Had that man already broken out of his painful twisted body and become free? I want him alive even if he's broken and in pain. I want him to stay in this world where I live and breathe, where my daughters live and breathe, where my mother lives and breathes. No, I want him to be released from his pain as quickly as possible. The son had a vivid image of the man wrapped in bandages and lying in bed. That man was himself. He was that man. No, no, it wasn't true, he wasn't that man at all. These were his thoughts while the woman accused him. What the hell was that man to him? Had a woman also accused that man of being a demon and a destroyer? Still holding his daughter, his eyes blurred with tears. The man was huge. He could hear the man's voice calling his brother. The flames rose. Each time they did, a voice called out in the crowd. The man could feel the brother staring at him. Fire puts people in a trance. The man patted the brother's head. I'm the one who released the flames, but the instant fire leaves my hand, it moves of its own accord and devours everything in its path. To him this was the mystery of fire. "Hey, little brother," the man bent down whispering into the brother's ear, "You go back to your mother's place. I've got some business to take care of at Hide's. You just wait till tomorrow."

The man took his hand from the brother's shoulder and nudged him forward.

"Hey, if you don't listen when I tell you to go home, I'll wop you. Your mother's pregnant, you should be with her."

The man walked away. He took a road off the road that led in front of Yatsuhashi's. Ueda no Hide's house was just around a bend to the right. Actually, the house was no longer Ueda no Hide's. Better to call it Kinoe's house. Ueda no Hide had long since gotten together with another woman and moved on, leaving it to her. Seeing the man's face, Kinoe said, "Another huge fire."

"Leave it alone," said the man. "Fires happen in a small town like this where people live all on top of each other like fuckin' sardines." He took a wad of money out of his pocket and gave her half.

"Are you sure? So much?" Kinoe asked. "You don't have to give it to the boy's mother or to the girl with long hair? I know all about it, the girl with the long hair, she's pregnant too."

"Yeah, yeah, don't give me a lot of shit about it. If you whore yourself now, your baby's goin' to die."

"What a funny man you are. What did you expect, getting three women pregnant at the same time? The boy's mother's going to be mad. I don't care, I'm having the child because I want it. But the boy's mother is different, she expects to settle down with you. The girl's the same. I don't know what sweet words you used to trick her, but she thinks you're the only one for her. She believes it. Now that would be amusing, wouldn't it, if you got all three of us pregnant women together, there'd be quite a scene. Even more amusing than one of your fires."

"Shut up, bitch."

"Why should I?"

"Because I say so."

"Why, why do I have to shut up? Did I do something wrong?"

"Aw, you haven't done anything wrong," said the man giving in. He bit into a dried persimmon that Kinoe's younger sister had brought from the mountains.

"Even if the three women fight, you won't suffer, Yasu. It's the three children who are going to have a hard time of it. They'll be brother and sister but they won't be together, they're bound to scatter. If the three babies turn out fine, why don't you see if you can introduce them to each other. Then at least they'll know what their siblings look like."

"Idiot," said the man.

The brother went straight home. The house was dark. He opened the door. Behind him the barley in the field was swaying. Suddenly he felt his own father was standing behind him trying to enter the house, and he looked over his shoulder. Nobody was there. Just as the man had said, a house is made of paper and wood. But this house was neither his father's house nor the man's house; it was his mother's house. Here the mother had gotten pregnant and given birth. It was her nest. He imagined the house in flames. If it burns down, we'll just build it again, he whispered to himself. Silently, the brother got into bed.

ॐ

"Where was the fire, boy?" the uncle asked.

"Yatsuhashi," he answered.

There were no more questions. If that man is an arsonist, he wondered, will the baby in my mother's belly be an arsonist too? If that man is a murderer, will the baby be a murderer? He felt the sting of regret. It was too late now, but if his mother had to get pregnant, she could have chosen a decent, kind, good person who wouldn't hurt others, and they could have really worked together. That guy is evil, a devil, he sets houses on fire without thinking, he beats people up without thinking, he wears that same could-care-less look even when he kills a dozen people, he's bad, he causes grief, he creates hell around him, he doesn't understand how much work it takes to build houses of paper and wood. He destroys them without thinking, just burns them down all the same, even enjoys doing it.

The son ruminated. That man's skull was cracked, his face crushed, his ribs broken.

Red Hair

The woman's hair was a reddish blond. Lifeless and fake-looking. The color suited her rough skin. She was pale skinned, but she hadn't always been that way. She looked as if she'd once had a deep tan from the sun and then lightened when she stopped going outdoors. The redhead was eating, her mouth grinding up and down slowly, her hair bouncing. She wasn't wearing anything under her slip, so her whole body could be seen to move as she chewed purposefully, her black nipples visible through the fabric. After she finished her meal, she looked up at Kōzō as if she'd just noticed him there.

"What?" she asked.

The woman stared hard into Kōzō's eyes as he lay on his stomach on the futon. "You mean this?" she smiled, hitching up her slip. Her stiff black pubic hair came into view. The smell of her crotch still hovered around him.

The woman stood, picking up the bowl and chopsticks she'd been using. She deposited them noisily in the sink and turned on the tap. The sound of running water drowned out the noise of the rain outside.

"Hey, move over."

The woman burrowed into Kōzō's futon, her elbow pressing into his side. "I'm so cold," she said, hugging his naked chest with cold arms and wrapping her feet around him. Pressed against his stomach, the woman's slip felt cold from the air outside. Her red hair, dyed like a doll's, loomed up close. Soon he could feel the warmth of her skin.

Sensing the woman's abdomen expanding with every breath, he shifted a little and slid his finger up behind her until he felt her cunt. The woman raised her hips. He didn't plan on doing it again. Since the woman had landed in his apartment, he'd had sex with her for three straight days and his pubic bone ached sweetly. He also felt a languorous sensation in his groin, almost a kind of dementia, from bumping up against the woman so many times.

He'd picked the woman up at a bus stop beyond the pass carved out of the mountains not far from the next station down the line. Since that day they'd been together in Kōzō's apartment.

The naked woman's nipples were black.

"I got two kids," she said.

The older one was four, the younger three. Both boys.

Kōzō stroked the woman's pubic hair. Even though he wrapped it around and around his finger, it sprang back straight it was so wiry.

The woman, kissing Kōzō's chest, lifted her head and looked at him with wet lips.

"Y'ever do speed?" she asked.

With the back of his finger Kōzō started to stroke the folds of skin, which opened like the petals of a flower. Maybe because of the pleasure she felt, she gave him a white, toothy smile. "They say it works if you put it down there."

"Speed?"

Next door to Kōzō lived a couple who shot up "shabu," a street-variety speed. The husband, about forty with sunken cheeks, had done too much of the drug and now heard voices, while his wife, a young beauty with clear eyes—an odd match for him—often screamed out in the middle of the night at the top of her lungs. To her listeners it sounded like a rage that had been pent up so long she couldn't hold onto it anymore, and just had to unleash it. Each scream would end in a long wail. Kōzō had gotten used to it, but the screams had shocked the redhead and made her shake Kōzō out of sleep. Kōzō explained that the neighbor always lost it in the middle of the night because of the shabu, and the woman accepted this.

"How about you?" Kōzō asked, curious about how much she knew.

The woman said she had a friend who'd gone out with a young guy and then drowned herself after becoming an addict. When they pulled the body out of the water, her toes were bent all the way back, maybe from the trauma of drowning or from the ecstasy of being high—there were needle marks all across her body. "Like this," the woman showed him, bending back her fingers. He could just see the water dripping through her fingers.

The woman ran her tongue over Kōzō's bud-sized nipples. The cunt he'd been stroking with his finger would now be red and engorged, he thought, its folds slippery wet. The woman put her hand on Kōzō's stomach and teasingly stroked the area around his cock. As her hair brushed against his face, Kōzō could smell a mixture of perfumed hair oil and sour blood. The woman pushed off the covers and tried to guide Kōzō's fingers into her, twisting her body. She closed her eyes. A steady drip sounded, indicating a sharp rise of water in the gutters.

⚘

On the fourth day after the woman had come to his apartment, Kōzō cautioned her to stay indoors and keep out of sight, and then he left for work. The construction company Kōzō worked for had an office next to a bridge spanning the canal that ran through the center of town.

The rain was really a light mist, but it continued to fall steadily. Kōzō poked his head in at the office and, while waiting for a truck to be assigned to him, he cornered Takao, who was just about his age, and together they went to a coffee shop. He would have preferred to talk about the redhead who was living in his apartment, but he willed himself not to, and talked instead about how slippery the main road by the river had gotten with all the rain. Takao said that the previous morning he had seen two accidents there, one after another. In the first accident, the left side of a truck had slid into a ditch on the mountain and gotten wedged there. In the second, it looked as if the truck had overturned and slammed hard into the mountainside, because there was shattered glass all over and gasoline leaking out. With the wind coming off the river, though, the fumes were blown away and the truck didn't catch on fire.

"The driver was sitting there on the grass right nearby holding a cigarette in his mouth," Takao said incredulously, adding that he had yelled at the man about the risk of fire. When the driver, smeared with gas and dirt and wearing only one shoe, finally noticed that somebody was yelling at him, he waved, limped over, and, completely composed, asked to be taken to a phone. After Takao guided him into the front passenger seat, the driver, who reeked of alcohol, took a cigarette out of his pocket and lit it from the truck's lighter without missing a beat.

The plum tree visible from the coffee shop had completely lost its petals.

Kōzō had seen his share of accidents, too. More often, students with backpacks and girls going to school asked him for rides as he drove every day along the highway that ran from the river into the mountains or down the road by the sea. Company rules said you couldn't give a ride to anyone who wasn't an employee, but the five drivers all ignored the rules and gave rides as the mood took them.

Until very recently that spring they'd been transporting gravel from the river to a factory making concrete that would be used for building a port two stations down the line. The concrete factory belonged to the construction company Kōzō worked for, but since spring Kōzō's division had started taking on contract work and was able to stand on its own. They were now like a heavy equipment rental company. The five drivers weren't happy about this, but because they had trailer licenses and other special permits in addition to their truck licenses, they could fill the need of any small company that didn't have its own drivers and equipment. The boss called them the ninja unit.

The days when a laborer rhythmically dug a hole and mixed cement with a shovel were over. In three to four hours an excavator could do the work of five men working three days. Shovels and picks were no longer tools of the trade; all you had to do was touch up the hole carved out by the excavator and the bulldozer, keeping an eye on the plans. Instead of swinging a pick, you pulled a handle. The boss said he was keeping his five invincible ninja and acquiring lots of equipment because the company had so much capital, and though the drivers loved cruising around in trucks, they hated being sent out by the company to operate excavators and bulldozers at other work sites.

Once when Kōzō took a bulldozer to a crew that had contracted for it a young worker there was fascinated by the sight of the equipment at work. "Anybody can learn this fast," Kōzō told him and then taught him how to operate the machine. The worker learned quickly enough, but later the boss scolded Kōzō and lectured him long and hard on the difference between leasing the equipment by itself and leasing it with a driver. The practice of leasing a machine with a driver had been an attempt to streamline and modernize the inefficient system used by the fifty or so contractors in the town. But to Kōzō, who didn't understand the first thing about business plans and modernization, the boss's lecture went in one ear and out the other.

Takao got up from his seat and said he was going to check on the truck assignment. When he returned a little later, he had a smile on his face.

"No orders today."

He sat down again and picked up the sports newspaper he'd been reading.

"Tell me about all this capital we have. If the workers have a day off, so do I."

Watching Takao's eyes narrow as he smiled, Kōzō thought of the redhead in the apartment with the rain falling softly outside. He felt a fire spreading through his loins, and at the sight of his own reflection in the glass he recalled the woman's tongue tirelessly licking his tired cock that would ache when it grew erect. Pulling the woman on top of him and pressing his soft member against her, he asked her if it didn't hurt doing it over and over again, and she stared into his eyes, licked the saliva off his lips, and whispered with a smile that yes, it hurt.

Flaccid without her touch, Kōzō couldn't penetrate the woman's wet, sore cunt. With her chest pressed to his naked chest, she raised her hips and wriggled, trying to get the soft floppy tip into her body.

"So you fucked your husband this much too?"

The woman snorted her assent, and this excited him, and she finally pushed his stiffening cock inside of her saying, "Yes, again and again and again." Her tongue tasted of semen to him, and the woman told him, "You taste like that, too." He could smell a yeasty smell as if he'd breathed in flour. Watching his own reflection in the window, he realized that what the woman gazed at, the fluids she licked, and the saliva she swallowed were all the stuff of his own body.

Takao smiled at the sight of the painful bulge in Kōzō's pants as his friend shifted uneasily in his seat.

Saying if there weren't any orders he was taking the day off, Kōzō went straight home. The woman with red hair was in his apartment.

"There you are, you're early," called the woman as if she had been greeting him every day. The futon was still spread out on the floor but she must have tidied up the scattered magazines and the dirty socks and underwear because the room looked in order. The window had been thrown open, and a hand's breadth away a white rain was falling.

The woman had gotten dressed. She wore the same clothes she was wearing when Kōzō picked her up in his dump truck, but they still looked fresh. The woman sat on the edge of the futon. "You can see a lot from here," she said. After Kōzō stripped off his sweater and was down to his shirt sleeves, the woman said under her breath, "I didn't think you'd be back till this evening, so I was just sitting here daydreaming."

Kōzō closed the window. In nothing but a shirt he found the room chilly. Usually, by this time he'd be on his way to a pachinko parlor, or he'd be meeting up with friends and going to a favorite coffee shop to bother the girls.

"Hungry?" asked the woman. "Just now when I was staring out the window, I remembered a delicious noodle shop just over there where the department store set up that big balloon."

"You can get good noodles anywhere."

The redhead gave a hint of a smile.

"Actually, I made some a little while ago and ate them."

Kōzō shivered with the cold and the woman peered into his

eyes as if trying to read his mood, saying in a small voice, "Let's go to bed."

They got into bed and the woman snuggled up to his naked flesh, put Kōzō's hand between her legs and breathed into his ear, "See how wet I am." After Kōzō had gone to work the woman hadn't been able to stand it and she had masturbated, she told him. Her nipples had been tingling painfully. A flame that had lain extinguished and forgotten in her body raged over her soft flesh, and unable to bear the smell of socks, under-wear, and the musty scent of a man in the room, she had gen-tly stimulated herself. Pressing her naked body against his and seeming to bask in the warmth, the woman said, "If you didn't come back tonight I was going to find somebody else to keep me warm," and then she raised herself up to pull Kōzō down on top of her. Lying beneath Kōzō, the woman lifted up her feet, raised her hips, and yelled out in abandon when Kōzō entered her. Her voice traveled from her womb which bore his weight, through her gut, and up into her stomach, and she moaned as if that part of her body were giving her pain. Because Kōzō had sucked on her breasts, the woman's nipples were wet with saliva as if they were still leaking milk, and a rich black in color. One of her breasts fit into the palm of his hand. As he felt her body contracting hard around him, Kōzō wondered how many men the woman had welcomed this way. Had the woman's husband fucked her this way every night, maybe even abused her? Kōzō came almost at the same time as the woman and, in the middle of a climax that felt like a burst of anger, Kōzō guessed that the woman's husband was behind the color of her lusterless red hair and had taught her everything she knew. She had shown Kōzō how to fuck in a sitting position, her ankles on his shoulders, but as he watched her watch his penis slide in and out and let out a cry, Kōzō realized that it was the husband who had taught her how to increase her pleasure by twisting her hips back and forth to tighten her hold.

As he stroked the woman's spasming stomach and ran his hands down her sides, Kōzō guessed that the man who taught the woman about pleasure must live somewhere near the bus stop on the other side of the pass. The woman's eyelids were wet with tears.

Kōzō got up, wet a towel, wrung it out hard, wiped the woman between the legs, and briskly scrubbed the futon where fluid had gushed out of her body. Just as he was about to wipe his own groin, the woman brushed away his hand with a "no" and, with Kōzō still in a squatting position, she put her red head between his legs, pushed her nose against his shrunken balls, and pressed her lips to them. She had kicked off the covers, and was lying on her back, pushing herself up on her arms. Like a dog, she licked from his balls to his anus, holding Kōzō tightly by the ankles, her nails digging into his flesh. Following the woman's wishes, Kōzō braced himself to stay in a squat, and he dropped forward on to his elbows to keep his balance above her. Moving with him, the woman tried to suck both of his balls at the same time. Watching the curtain of red hair shake, he rubbed her crotch with the twisted towel. Maybe the husband who'd made her dye her hair had done the same thing, too. No, he might have gently rubbed the lips that open like the petals of a flower, but he'd almost certainly never twisted the towel into a screw shape and put it inside of her. Opening the woman's legs and pressing his lips to her, Kōzō laughed bitterly at his own childishness.

❦

It was Kōzō who finally asked the woman to go out with him. He didn't understand why she stayed on in his apartment, and he couldn't figure out his own feelings about her. He wasn't seeing anybody else, so he had no reason to feel she was a bother, but he didn't feel he just had to be with her, or that he was madly in love with her. One day simply turned into three, and three days stretched into four. In the thin misting rain, Kōzō put an umbrella over the woman and they headed to the shopping district by a back street.

The woman put her arm through his, clinging to him.

"Do you hurt?" he asked, putting his mouth to her ear.

"A little," she answered with a serious look, gazing off into the rain.

Kōzō could smell the woman's scent emanating from his own body. Right behind the shopping arcade was a coffee shop. "I haven't changed my underwear. I can't go on forever like this," the woman said, and then pointing at the coffee shop, she told him to wait for her there. He asked her if she had any money and she said, "I have a little. . . ." Kōzō gave her ten thousand yen.

Under the eaves of the coffee shop, Kōzō handed her the umbrella.

"I'll be back in a minute, so wait for me," said the woman with a vacant stare, and then she walked away. She said she hurt, but from her walk she looked like any other woman.

The woman returned after about an hour. Her arms were full of shopping bags and she showed him a pair of thick green curtains with a pattern of bold brown lines.

"I got this far before I realized I forgot to buy curtain rods, but it doesn't matter. We can hang them on nails and use them right away."

The woman peered into the bag and told Kōzō that she'd also bought teacups and chopsticks, plus a handy-sized stew pot. The red hair with its slight wave shook in time to the woman's fast speech.

"You buy yourself some panties?"

At Kōzō's question, the look in the woman's eyes changed completely.

"Want to see?" she asked. Conscious of Kōzō's lewd laugh, she rustled around in the bags, then placed one bag in front of Kōzō and said, "This is for you." While holding another bag in her left hand she shifted the remaining bags from her knees to the floor. Her gesture vaguely reminded Kōzō of an insurance saleswoman he used to see. Even though he and the saleswoman had gone to a hotel together many times, she always clutched her hand-bag carefully in her lap and sat directly across from him. Just a little over thirty, she still had some time before her body began to thicken, but her behavior always reminded him of a middle-aged woman. The pollution of life had begun to cling to her like a habit that takes you over little by little unawares, and this aspect of her had had a certain erotic appeal that Kōzō didn't find in women his own age or younger. Whenever they had sex, the insurance woman raised her legs up in the air. As Kōzō moved violently on top of her, she held him tightly between her legs. She even grew anxious if she couldn't keep her legs up.

The redhead used a brittle white fingernail to painstakingly undo the tape on the folded bag. She rolled the tape in her hands into a little ball and then placed the bag on her lap again.

"These will make your head spin.... Look," said the woman, spreading one pair on the table. It was a shimmery peach color with green frills, and it looked like it was designed to fit a child. Kōzō chuckled, wondering whether the woman's tough pubic hair would pierce the fabric. At the sound of his laugh the woman suddenly realized they were in a coffee shop. She looked around, and when she saw the waiter watching them, she stuck out her tongue, shrank down in her seat, and nervously put the panties back in the bag.

"All men are perverts," she said, "with only one thing on their minds."

"Oh and what's that?" said Kōzō prompting her.

"Um," she whispered, shaking her head.

The woman was turning red. Most women Kōzō knew would have responded flippantly and not missed a beat: "If you don't know, I'll stick your nose right in it!"

Kōzō's girl cousin, who lived along the alleyways in the poorer part of town, had once stared at his friend Takao—who had been dumped by his girlfriend—and said to him with a straight face, "Huh, from the look of you I bet she went to find a real man instead of someone who looks like he can't get it up." Once, after Kōzō and about five of his friends had passed around a woman they'd picked up in town, this cousin and two of her girlfriends heard that one of the guys, not Takao, had ejaculated before even fucking her; a real loser, they called him, and treated him with scorn.

The redhead was different, thought Kōzō. Her unhealthy skin was flushed down to her neck, and she was looking at Kōzō with watery, unfocused eyes.

Outside the coffee shop, a white dog that looked like a Kishū breed trotted past.

They left the coffee shop and went to a grill-your-own pancake place on a back street between the shopping district and the movie house. Sitting on tatami mats in their own private room, Kōzō ordered a beer, and the woman ate the grilled cakes she had made, her red hair bouncing up and down. Chewing in her deliberate way, she held up her glass in her right hand to take the beer Kōzō was offering, and when she noticed the bottle was empty, she called out, "Miss, excuse me, one more beer please." The owner of the place walked over, her wooden sandals tapping on the floor; she slid open the door to the room and poked her head in. "Yes, what would you like?" she asked.

"Another beer," the woman said.

When the owner had slid the door shut, the woman said, "I feel like I'm eating real food for the first time."

ॐ

Kōzō didn't ask the woman anything about herself. There was no point. When you whistle at a strange dog and it follows you home, you can try to find out more about it, but in the end you have to decide whether to keep it or not. In the same way, Kōzō had only two choices—to let the woman stay on in his apartment or send her home. The redhead stayed.

After the woman came to live with him, Kōzō marveled at how much life had changed. In the past he rarely ate a meal off dishes in his own apartment, but now there were new dishes sitting covered by a dishcloth. A red plastic rope had been stretched across the bottom half of the window, and clothes were drying there. From the door frame hung a woman's red apron and a blouse. These few objects immediately brightened up the room. Kōzō's apartment, which lacked even a television or a stereo and had simply been a place to sleep, was looking more and more like the apartments of his friends and coworkers. Since the woman had come to live with him, Kōzō was amazed by how much her little touches had changed things. The woman, for her part, showed a fascination with all the details of a bachelor's life.

At dawn the redhead seemed to listen without fail for the cry of the shabu addict as if it were the refrain of her new life. "Listen," she'd say as the voice sounded, often waking Kōzō. To Kōzō, it was a noise as familiar as the squeal of a pig. He didn't feel a thing. The only reason to maybe get disturbed by it was that the addicts were basically people like themselves, but if the screams were disturbing then so were the cries of all the women at night from the surrounding apartments. Kōzō didn't take the position that moans of pleasure from his house were fine, while those of other people were bad. He simply didn't notice how loud the redhead's cries were, because for years now he'd been hearing the cries of the women around him through the thin walls of the apartment building. Whenever the woman told him to listen to the woman addict, he'd say, "She's squealing like a pig because it just feels so good." Maybe she'd just shot up and was feeling giddily ecstatic about being alive. Once he was awake, Kōzō would massage the woman's breasts and bring her to a climax, or he'd fall back to sleep with the woman bending over him. The woman seemed to want Kōzō to play with her constantly, as if the only thing she really needed was pleasure that assaulted her body over and over again in waves.

They'd been having sex, licking and caressing each other all over, until just before they'd left the house that day, but then the woman lowered her voice in the next place they went into and whispered to Kōzō, "I want to do it again."

"Sure," Kōzō replied. "We'll fuck again later and take our time."

On one occasion Kōzō came home to find the woman lying naked in bed. Her eyes looked watery. For a moment Kōzō imagined that the redhead had let another man into his apartment and had had sex with him, and because he didn't know exactly how to accuse her, he said, "I'm off all day at work and you don't even make dinner? Shit. I need a woman who can cook, so you got to go." When he turned the woman out of the futon and saw her wearing his underwear, he was flustered. The redhead got up, put her face in her hands, and wept, her whole body shaking.

Ⓖ

Once the woman had completely taken over his apartment, Kōzō noticed how her scent filled the air. And it wasn't a bad thing. The apartment of a twenty-eight-year-old man should smell like a woman, not like some baseball locker room or nondescript dusty office. The room filled with the smells of the woman's secretions, her red hair, her makeup, her nail polish remover. A yeasty smell hovered around Kōzō's nostrils.

The woman said it was Kōzō's smell. When Kōzō contradicted her, she spoke as though she were an expert in matters of love: "A bachelor has a special smell. Little by little it's been fading and I can't pin it down, but you still have a special odor."

"Ah, I see you know all about it," he teased her.

"I might be living from hand to mouth, but I'm not stupid," she said.

"But it's been coming from you since you got here. I've been wondering what it was the whole time," he said.

Her voice softened at the confused look on his face. "You wouldn't know about it, but somebody who's slept with you would."

The face of the insurance saleswoman floated up in front of Kōzō.

One day when Kōzō came home from work the woman told him she'd seen the shabu addicts. She'd been hanging clothes on the plastic line to dry when she felt somebody staring at her from below. She looked out the window, and a skinny woman was glaring up at her. It might have been someone out looking for her so she shrank back. From below, the skinny woman yelled something. The redhead couldn't make out what she was saying, but she recognized the addict's voice. Plucking up her courage, she peered out the window again. Then the addict turned toward her and began yelling, "I'm going to kill you!" As if agitated by the sound of her own voice, the addict marched up to the redhead's apartment door and started banging on it. "Come out, I'm going to kill you!" she shouted, still deluded and entirely unconcerned about what the neighbors might think of her.

A couple living in the same building finally contacted the woman's husband. He was able to mollify his wife, and together the two walked back toward the window where the voice usually came from. The redhead didn't say much more about the incident, but she was clearly shocked by the addict's threat to murder her the very first time they met. For a long while after the addict went home, the woman couldn't think of anything to do, and she waited for Kōzō's return, struggling with a feeling of anxiety that nearly made it hard for her to breathe. To calm her down, Kōzō pulled her close, took off a few of her clothes, and carefully stroked her and kissed her intently until she gave a cry that came from deep inside her. After the daylight had faded completely, he took her to his cousin's house.

A couple who ran a kimono mail order business was also there visiting the cousin. The redhead fell silent and sat behind Kōzō, doing her very best to avoid eye contact. In the brief interval when the redhead went to the bathroom, Satoko, the cousin, twisted a finger counterclockwise in the air, saying, "She's crazy, right?" It was too much trouble for Kōzō to explain from the beginning, so he just nodded agreeably. Satoko slapped Kōzō on the thigh and then, with one hand over her mouth, laughed silently, "Shame on you!" The woman returned from the bathroom and sat down again behind Kōzō.

"I have the feeling I've seen you somewhere before," said the skinny man who ran the kimono mail order business.

"Hmm, now that you mention it, I've been thinking the same thing," agreed Fuki, Satoko's half sister, who was ten years her senior.

"Hey, say, weren't you living around Owase until recently?"

"I'm not familiar with that area," the woman whispered.

"Back beyond Ōsato, even deeper in the mountains. I think you came to see my samples at a show when I drove up there with a bunch of stuff."

The woman shook her head.

"Must have been somebody else, then," said Fuki simply and then changed the topic in an attempt to turn the conversation back to her husband. "Driving all over the country with those samples, you get into all sorts of interesting situations, right, Papa?"

"I don't know how it is in your family, Kōzō, but in ours, Mama calls the shots," the man rasped, a smile coming to his lips, as if it didn't bother him in the least because she always teased him this way. "I don't drive too good, so I sit next to Mama, and if I tell her hey, all this jostling is making me horny, she calls me a lazy slob. But when she gets all hot and bothered, she doesn't give a shit about how I feel. Like that time we got to the motel where we were staying and she says to me, 'I'm going in right now, got it?' and she barges in the front door before I can get a word in edgewise."

The man waved at her with a hand missing its little finger. The gesture made the story seem even more like their own invention. The man, who'd been a racketeer, had gone to collect a debt and beaten someone up when things didn't go his way. He'd been serving time in jail for assault.

"We could've taken a bath in the motel together, but I was worried 'cause I'd been messing around with some girl the day before and maybe I got a hickey somewhere, see, so I go into the bath first to check, and boy am I relieved to see I'm clean. So I wash myself fast and get out. On my way out, I meet this one going in. She's mumbling under her breath. 'You were out last night screwing around, and I'm gonna strangle you and get off on doing it.' I'm a man, O.K.? but I'm bracing myself and I'm waiting and waiting for her to come out of the bath, but still she doesn't come."

"It was such a big bath, wasn't it," said Fuki.

"About the size of three tatami mats. Anyway, I go in and there she is in the bathroom, all lathered up from head to toe and doing a soap dance. What a sight!"

Satoko gave a chuckle and asked, "So then you did a soap dance together?"

"You bet, we did."

Satoko laughed and clapped her hands together. The redhead didn't laugh.

"There right over the wall was a sign explaining how to soap your partner all over, and since that's what Mama ordered...I felt like I was working at a Turkish bath, and I blew bubbles and serviced my customer at the same time."

They'd gone to the motel during one of Ōsato's floods when they thought they wouldn't be able to reach the exhibition hall. Two days later, the water receded and they left to attend another show some distance from Owase toward the coast. Located between a swamp and a river, Ōsato had had lousy drainage for the past fifty years, so the water always rose however little or much it rained. The woman who resembled the redhead lived there, they said.

"Did she have the red hair?"

"I only have a vague memory. But who cares if she was there or not? You know the gardens of the houses up there look like riverbeds with stones lying all over the place," said Fuki standing up. "That must be tough."

"Ōsato, huh? You know that little restaurant where we all met the other day, the guy who runs it is from there," said Satoko. And then, growing serious, she turned to the woman and said soothingly, "We're not checking up on you, you know."

Without attracting the attention of the others, the woman was stroking Kōzō's buttock with one finger.

Kōzō had picked up the redhead in his truck on the road heading toward the coast in the opposite direction of Ōsato, so he didn't believe what Fuki and the man were saying. To get from there to Ōsato, you had to cross Yanoko Pass. On the way home from Satoko's house, the woman wept. But Kōzō had no interest in finding out about the woman's past. All he needed was a warm body.

The woman washed her tear-streaked face at the sink and dried it with a towel, and a few minutes later spoke in a voice that sounded as if it was someone else who had been weeping so pitifully. "The supermarket on the corner had a sale on instant ramen, so I bought a whole lot of it. You want me to make you some?"

Without waiting for Kōzō's answer, she put water on to boil.

"When you get your next paycheck, we need a new gas range. This one always dies when I light it. People always call me spacey, but I'd hate to get burned by this finicky thing. The way I am, I don't notice when it goes out," said the woman.

The woman took two packages of ramen out of a brown paper bag and opened them, and then mumbled as if the observation had just occurred to her, "That supermarket is cheap.... The eggs are dirt cheap, and that chocolate on a stick is two or three yen cheaper than the other places."

"Two or three yen, huh?" said Kōzō, prompting her.

"The people around here don't realize it, but shopping is cheap here. You know why the eggs in the supermarket are so cheap? Did you know there's a chicken farm right near here?"

"Yeah, and a pig farm too, only a five-minute walk from here," said Kōzō.

"It's ready," said the woman carrying a bowl of ramen in both hands and setting it down in front of Kōzō. "Here you go," she said, handing him chopsticks. Then she brought over her own bowl filled with ramen from the pot and set it down in front of Kōzō, too.

"You know today when I went to the supermarket, I couldn't decide whether to buy eggs or not, and when I didn't get them, my luck went bad. With even just one egg, it doesn't taste instant, does it."

The woman sucked up the broth. As he watched the woman's hair tremble, Kōzō wondered if the same man owned both the supermarket around the corner and the chicken farm.

✿

With her warm tongue, the woman licked Kōzō's face from his stubbly chin to his cheek over and over again. When his cheek was itchy and wet with her saliva, he put his hand behind her hair and pulled her lips to his. He forced his tongue between her lips and stroked her hair as she sucked at Kōzō's saliva like a baby at the breast. With the point of his tongue, he explored hers. The woman pressed back at him so hard that their teeth bumped. One of her hands was digging into his anus. She wanted to be licked like a dog, to lick like a dog. Her tongue traveled ravenously over the goosebumps on Kōzō's naked body. Kōzō held open the lips of her cunt with one finger and softly moved his tongue over her, blowing air into her most delicate parts. The woman pressed her lips to Kōzō's pubic hair and bit down, wetting the hair with her saliva, and cried out again. He'd heard her give that wrenching cry so many times, but it was still new to him. The same voice out of the same body, but to Kōzō it seemed he was hearing this cry of pleasure for the first time. With her torso pinned down from above, the woman stretched out her legs, opening them as wide as she could, and then once she'd reached the limits of her strength, she closed her legs, saying, "No." As she lay there drained of strength, the woman rubbed Kōzō's head while he continued to play with her. Feeling the touch of the woman's hand on his head, Kōzō placed his cheek against her, savoring the warmth of her body as waves of pleasure washed over her. She didn't try to push his weight off her but breathed raggedly, finally asking him to hold her in the normal way, and grumbling, "I'm all sweaty, aren't I?" Kōzō got up. The woman had drained him of all moisture and he felt thirsty. Still with an erection, he went to the sink, put his mouth to the tap, and drank. The dark sink smelled of warm food, a smell it had never had before.

"Want a drink?" Kōzō asked the woman.

Suddenly worn out, the woman covered herself, bringing her legs together and bending them, and said, "I am thirsty." Kōzō filled his mouth from the tap again; keeping sight of the woman's watery eyes upon him, he swished the water around in his mouth as if gargling and came over to the woman. She didn't laugh. Dead serious, she stretched her hands up to Kōzō, who stood over her looking down, and grasped him by the ankles so he wouldn't look away. Still watching her, Kōzō squatted and held her by the head like a fresh trophy. When the woman raised her upper body he passed the warm water into her mouth, taking care not to spill. The woman drank with gusto. The warm water spilled out of her lips, down her chin, and flowed through the cleft in her breasts.

Observing the traces of water on her skin, Kōzō asked, "What's it taste like?"

The woman clicked her tongue, tilted her head in thought, and smiled back at him. "Instant ramen."

Kōzō laughed, and the woman reached out and touched his penis as he knelt before her; still in a sitting position she opened her legs and raised them, inviting him to enter her. Kōzō sat down on the futon ready to oblige. Slowly, the woman placed both feet on his shoulders. This was her favorite position. Kōzō pressed his fully erect penis into the woman. The sheets were wet with her fluid or the water she'd spilled there. A smell of yeast pervaded the air again. The woman was wet enough, but Kōzō had trouble getting his penis in. She leaned forward as if she couldn't wait anymore, worked him inside her, and then, as if she had just realized how big and threatening he looked, she stared into his eyes fearfully, saying, "You frightened me just then—like you were making me drink poison."

Kōzō squeezed both of the woman's black nipples between his fingers.

"I don't know why but you were scary."

The woman's voice sounded as if it were coming from the base of her spine, and he thrust himself deep inside her in the direction of that voice. The woman shook her red hair, arched back, and raised her hips moving back and forth and side to side. The nipples on her arched chest gleamed blackly, and he fucked her hard to impress himself on those two nipples that had been sucked on by her teacher-husband and her two kids. She shook her red hair, and Kōzō felt a hot flame coursing through his body as he listened to her cries. Was it hatred of the others who had sucked on those breasts, or was it his own lust ignited by the woman and growing hotter and hotter. He didn't know.

The woman had closed her eyes and was tossing her hair; then she let out a scream, squeezing him tightly between her legs. It occurred to Kōzō again that he didn't like this position, and he took her feet down from his shoulders.

Once in Kōzō's arms, the woman finally seemed to recognize his presence, and she put her arms around his neck, pressed her breasts to his chest, and kissed his face. While making the woman suck on his tongue, Kōzō carefully maneuvered the woman's body beneath him so as not to slip out of her. He felt his abdomen trembling with the effort.

The light seemed too clinical, so Kōzō reached over and pulled the cord, maintaining his position on top. As if she'd been waiting for the room to plunge into darkness, the woman released his tongue and began licking his nose as if it were a penis. Kōzō stroked her stiff pubic hair, and with her legs open and raised, he thrust into her hard. He didn't care if he ripped her womb to shreds if it was for his own pleasure; he would even strangle her. Kōzō and his buddies had read a bizarre story in a magazine about a man who couldn't forget the sensation he'd had during sex while strangling a woman, so he went around raping and killing. The woman cried out. She was moaning as if she couldn't take much more, rubbing her sperm-filled crotch up against Kōzō, and she dug her nails into his buttocks as if to say deeper, harder, but that wasn't enough, so she grabbed his ass and pushed a finger up his anus trying to force it open. Feeling the pain of the flesh tearing under her nails and the tight way she gripped him, he ejaculated into her long and hard.

With all his weight on her, Kōzō waited for the blue white flame in his body to die down. The flame crackled.

The red-haired woman pushed Kōzō off and without saying a word dived for his crotch. Then as if it were the most natural thing in the world, she sat on his face. In the darkness, the woman's buttocks loomed up before Kōzō's eyes. He didn't mind; he stroked the flesh between her hole and her anus, rubbing her with his stubbly beard. Sweat appeared in the woman's crack.

The woman moved up his body, kissing him from his stomach to his chest, and then she pressed her soft warm lips against his. Slipping her tongue into his mouth, she moved it around, exchanging saliva. Kōzō sucked the sharp-tasting saliva into his mouth. She reached down to his groin, rubbed the tip of

his penis, and whispered into Kōzō's ear, "Let's do it all night."
Kōzō stroked the woman's hair with both hands. She stroked
his penis, pressed her lips to his, and pushed her tongue into
his mouth sucking hard. Pulling away, she breathed into his
ear, "Look it's hard again," and then said, "I can't forget you."
She gave him a love bite on the ear, climbed on top of him,
raised the hand that was stroking her hair, and, pressing her
nose into his armpit, she kissed him.

ॐ

The shabu addict let out a scream that ended in a long wail. That
morning it was Kōzō who woke up first to the sound. The woman's head lay on Kōzō's chest, and her hand rested near his pubic
hair as if she could never get enough of him. The curtains were
drawn, but from the noise in the gutters he knew rain was falling
in the growing white light. Again, he heard the addict scream
like a pig rutting for food, but he couldn't decide if it was in rage
or despair. The woman slept on.

Kōzō lifted the red hair off the woman's face as she slept naked,
and suddenly he felt it was a mercy that the sky was white instead
of a deep blue that would wake you up with a start. The rain went
pitter-patter in the gutters.

Trying not to wake her, Kōzō disentangled himself and got
up, put his mouth to the tap, and drank. Then he filled the kettle with water and placed it on the gas range just as the woman
did every morning. After he lit the burner, he watched the blue
flames for a while, but feeling his cock go hard and heavy and
raise its head, he turned the kettle down low. He tried to get the
flame low enough so that the water would boil in about an hour
but a small wind wouldn't blow it out. But maybe he didn't need
to boil water. His groin was tingling. On silent feet, Kōzō crossed

over to the window and looked out of a chink in the curtains; a mistlike rain was falling from the sky, and he could see the water from the gutter draining into the concrete ditch below.

The woman had turned over in her sleep and was curled up, her back and her bottom pointing toward Kōzō. He could see her cunt between two coarse, pure white moons. For a moment Kōzō squatted down next to her watching her sleep.

Kōzō woke the woman up because he heard the addict screaming again. When the woman realized that Kōzō was holding on to her from behind, she twisted around and planted a hard wet kiss on his lips, and then raised her chin at the sound of the screams.

"I dreamed I was high on speed," she said.

Kōzō opened her cunt with one finger. "Right...there," she said breathlessly. She pressed her legs to his, pushing herself up on top of him. Pressing her breasts against his chest, she leaned into Kōzō and whispered in his ear, "Last night I felt my legs bend all the way back."

As Kōzō stroked her dull red hair he felt a deep longing.

The woman glanced out the window. "Oh," she said, tilting her head, "it's raining again. We can stay in bed all day. But it's not always going to rain like this."

The woman with red hair pressed her lips to Kōzō's throat. Her lips were wet and unbelievably warm, thought Kōzō. The red hair shone.

Afterword

In his last interview before his death, Nakagami Kenji spoke about Akiyuki, the protagonist of a number of his early works. "Akiyuki is stirring again. He's the one who was closest to me and then moved so far away. Now it's just a matter of what form he's going to take."[1] While Nakagami enjoys a final dramatic performance here, playing with the boundaries between life and text, he is also speaking of his own death. The character of Akiyuki came into being in Nakagami's youth, the days when he boarded a train for Tokyo, spent his days in the jazz coffee shops and bars of Shinjuku, and wrote tough, bare stories about a place resembling his hometown of Shingū, Wakayama. In a moment of nostalgia, Nakagami revisits the strong young laborer, the one whose body never failed him.

Age forty-six and at the height of his literary career, Nakagami, at the time of this final interview, had written enough fiction and criticism to fill fifteen volumes of an edition of his collected works. Born in the outcaste neighborhood of Shingū in 1946, the young Kenji was the first in his family to "get letters," in his words, and his rise had been meteoric. A decade after his arrival in Tokyo in

---

[1] Nakagami Kenji, "Sporting with Illness," interview with Watanabe Naomi, *Bungakkai*, May 1992.

1965, Nakagami had become an innovative writer of fiction, a budding intellectual, and an outspoken critic of discrimination against minorities in Japan. His decline was meteoric, too: between the time he was diagnosed with kidney cancer and his death, less than a year had elapsed.[2]

In spite of his death in early middle age, Nakagami left a complex legacy to modern Japanese literature. No writer born after the war has taken the same risks that Nakagami did in terms of material, narrative voice, and literary style. Nakagami experimented with Japanese, pushing at the envelope of what the language could bear. In the early story, "The Cape," for example, he strips language down to create a sparse, disjointed style that disrupts the flow of narrative, taking us in and out of Akiyuki's head. Akiyuki crouches close to the ground, his ear attuned to the slightest changes in the natural world. Nakagami's language conveys the immediacy of his physical perceptions: "The night insects were just beginning to hum. If he listened hard he could hear them far away, like a buzzing in his ears" (p. 2). In his later work, Nakagami builds language back up little by little, creating wandering, dense sentences that curl inward upon themselves, sudden switches in point of view, and strange digressions. But in both early and later works, Nakagami deliberately eschews a polished literary style for what Iguchi Tokio has described as "chaotic sentence construction."[3] His rough-hewn style was both an assertion of difference, a defection from the literary center, and a challenge to what Karatani Kōjin describes as the "system" of modern Japanese literature.[4]

---

[2] See Takazawa Shūji's detailed chronology of Nakagami's life, *Nakagami Kenji Zenshū (Collected Works of Nakagami Kenji)*, vol. 15 (Tokyo: Shūeisha, 1996), pp. 739–89.

[3] Iguchi Tokio, *Monogatari-ron/ Hakyoku-ron (Theory of Narrative/ Theory of Trauma)* (Tokyo: Ronsōsha, 1987), p. 44.

[4] Karatani Kōjin, *Origins of Modern Japanese Literature*, trans. and ed. Brett de Bary (Durham: Duke University Press, 1993), p. 162.

The early works translated in this volume—"Misaki" (The Cape), "Kataku" (House on Fire), and "Akagami" (Red Hair)—are key to understanding Nakagami's fictional project. Seeds that will generate a whole oeuvre, the three stories show Nakagami to be a writer of Faulknerian preoccupations. The family relationships alone form a complex genealogy that passes from work to work. Nakagami further opens a world that most Japanese have never seen before—the *roji*, or "alleyways," the quarters of the *burakumin* (see the Translator's Preface, p. x). Nakagami takes his readers down into the "unclean" spaces of the alleyways, recording the local idiom of the laborer and fashioning a prose style that will capture the richness found there. In the character of Akiyuki, too, Nakagami experiments with a protagonist who does not "think" the world (like so many of the intellectualized protagonists of modern Japanese fiction) but rather one who allows the world to seep into his consciousness and to shape him.

These three formative stories also provide a window on Nakagami's preoccupation with the myriad forms of Japanese myth. In particular, Nakagami mounts a critique on certain beliefs that are seen to have shaped Japanese national consciousness—the sacred bloodline, the myth of a divine emperor (*tennōsei*), the story of the noble exile, the longing for purity, the worship of an animistic landscape. In his later work, Nakagami makes more pointed reference to the power and durability of myth by exhuming old tales, local legends, and stories and making fiction out of them in often startling and disjunctive ways. But we can date this interest in deconstructing myth to the very beginning of Nakagami's writing career.

Nakagami's preoccupation with the bloodline, for example, emerges in rough form in "House on Fire" and "The Cape" through the story of Akiyuki and his father. It is here that Nakagami first poses the question: who are the outcastes of Kishū? To illuminate the puzzle of outcaste identity, Nakagami draws upon the ancient Japanese "myth of the noble exile" (*kishuryūritan*), which tells the story of a noble or semi-divine youth who is cast out from his society and who must pass a number of trials before he can return home and succeed to the throne.⁵ Possibly holding a clue to the origins of the outcastes who wandered over the mountains and settled along the coast of Kishū, this story of abjection and apotheosis fascinates Nakagami. He begins to experiment with this theme through the story of the father, the strange drifter with unknown roots who assumes a semi-divine status as destroyer of the mother's "nest" and the matriarchal *roji*.⁶ By equating low and high, outcaste and noble, Nakagami's version of the "noble exile" story illuminates how extremes of low and high come into being, and how the need to keep such categories discrete results in discrimination (*sabetsu*), the oppression of one group by another.

Nakagami takes his reading of the myth of the noble exile even further, however: by creating a false patriarch, Nakagami parodies the myth of a sacred imperial male line—a myth that still survives in the figure of the emperor—and even calls into question belief in the nation itself. In his depiction of Akiyuki's tortured pursuit of his natural father, Nakagami suggests that although the sons of the *roji* are caught up in a blind longing for their fathers, they also understand that the question of succession is fundamentally a matter of belief. Driven by desire as he may be, Akiyuki is wary of depending on external sources

---

⁵ For a discussion of the myth see Haruo Shirane, *The Bridge of Dreams: A Poetics of the Tale of Genji* (Stanford: Stanford University Press, 1987), pp. 3–4.

⁶ In the later Akiyuki works—*Karekinada (Withered Tree Straits)*, 1977, and *Chi no Hate Shijō no Toki (The Sublime Time at the Ends of the Earth)*, 1982— Nakagami makes the link between outcaste and noble exile more explicit by creating a spurious ancestor, Magoichi, who descends from the mountains during wartime to establish a paradise for his descendants by the sea.

to shore up his identity. Insecurity plagues Akiyuki, but in the end, his ambivalent view of the patriarchy may be his greatest strength.

As he illuminates the advantage of the outsider, Nakagami also criticizes the belief in an authentic, transcendent self that remains a staple of modern Japanese fiction. In the Akiyuki series, the self does not spring into being ready for introspection and growth; rather, it has come through a difficult birth pressed by the forces of blood and geography, and often seems on the verge of dissolution. Akiyuki perceives his world through a fog of uncertainty and palpable anxiety. In his portrayal of Akiyuki, however, Nakagami does not mean to outline the vicissitudes of youth but to detail the friction and resistance experienced by the outcaste son who must carve out his own position with regards to family, to nation, and to self. The following sections trace the ways in which Nakagami creates this "friction" and how his protagonists reflect his own complex attitudes toward the self and the writing of fiction. As we move back into the mid 1970s, we return to the moment in Nakagami's career when Akiyuki first stirred and came into being.

The Cape

In January 1976 seven judges, including the writers Yasuoka Shōtarō, Yoshiyuki Junnosuke, and Niwa Fumio, awarded Nakagami one of the two Akutagawa Prizes for literature for his novella "The Cape" (published 1975). This literary award signaled Nakagami's debut as a serious writer on the Japanese literary scene. Even as they awarded him the prize, however, the judges' opinions were mixed. Five of the seven complained about the number of characters in "The Cape" and the difficulty of reading the work. Yet Yasuoka Shōtarō praised Nakagami's "sticking power and the strength of his pen," and Niwa Fumio praised the portrayal of the mother, the dialogue, and the style, stating that Nakagami had even "returned something to Japanese fiction (*shōsetsu*) that has been missing recently—the fiction (*shōsetsu*)."[7]

The judges' focus on Nakagami's energy and strength was echoed in discussions of his work in the national press. A review of "The Cape" in the *Asahi* newspaper in 1975 is representative in that it emphasizes the energy, rawness, and the sheer physicality of Nakagami's prose:

> [Nakagami's] the type who feverishly packs words full of the blood, sweat, anger, and shame of life that tingle (*uzuku*) inside him, and forges sentences with all his strength. . . . There doesn't seem to be much of an intellectual framework to his writing at least for now. But his prose has a unique strength, and he strikes one as being personable.[8]

Eto Jun, the literary critic, takes a similar tone in the *Mainichi Newspaper* when he reviews Nakagami's first longer novel, *Karekinada* (Withered Tree Straits), in 1977:

> . . . the prose in this longer work pulsates from beginning to end with the tingling (*uzuki*) of the writer's heart. . . . Reading *Karekinada*, I couldn't help feeling that after seventy years Japanese naturalism had finally fulfilled its promise. However, Nakagami's is not a borrowed naturalism;

[7] *Akutagawa-shō Zenshū (Collected Annals of the Akutagawa Prize)*, vol. 10 (Tokyo: Bungei Shunjū, 1982), pp. 437–42.
[8] *Asahi Newspaper*, 25 September 1975.

he creates characters through the pulse of his own heart
which drinks in earth and blood.... he is able to sing about
the pain people feel in this world.[9]

Both reviewers use the word *uzuku* (to tingle, to throb) to
describe the writings of the young Nakagami, whose fiction is
viewed as a cathartic release, not a cerebral exercise of craft. In
fact, the critics suggest that Nakagami is barely in control of his
own material, that he writes not in ink but in sweat and blood.
Unwittingly, these reviewers mark Nakagami as an outsider, a
country boy who was raised on heartier fare than the effete, intellectual products of Tokyo. One senses the critics flinching slightly
as if they have encountered a more primitive form of life.[10]

The sophistication, erudition, and difficulty of Nakagami's
work would become apparent in the 1980s, but one might forgive Nakagami's early readers for their focus on the visceral,
earthy side of his prose and their tendency to read the personality
through the fiction. Nakagami mined material from his own life
for the story of Akiyuki—the suicide of an older brother, a murder in his extended family, conflict with a biological father—and

---

[9] *Mainichi Newspaper*, 24 February 1977.

[10] The critical views of the blood-sweat-and-earth variety later produced a
backlash among Nakagami's contemporaries. In his 1987 study, the critic
Yomota Inuhiko, for example, lists a series of misinterpretations that should
be avoided when reading Nakagami's fiction: "locating details of the author's
life in the story of Akiyuki, feeling empathetic identification, seeing the
union of a young man with water, fire, the forces of nature, reading the return
of the gods to a godless world" (Yomota Inuhiko, *Kishu to Tensei* [Exile and
Return] [Tokyo: Shinchōsha, 1987], p. 158). Instead Yomota urges the reader
to consider Nakagami as a practiced writer of fictions who in each new work
is bent on criticizing and deconstructing the previous one. Karatani Kōjin
contradicts the blood-sweat-and-earth variety of criticism frequently, perhaps most poignantly at Nakagami's funeral in Tokyo when he claims in a
eulogy that "Nakagami was an intellectual writer, a more intellectual writer
than most."

by doing so, he blurred the line between life and fiction.[11] But again, this was a conscious strategy: by doing so, he would take his readers into the alleyway and lay the foundation for a fictional world that is astounding for its internal complexity and its ability to critique and revise itself over time.

"The Cape" tells the story of a family that gathers together to hold a memorial service for the first husband of the matriarch, the mother of Akiyuki. The son of a woman who has been married twice, but never to his natural father, Akiyuki grows up in the company of half-siblings from both marriages. One of these is Ikuo, a half-brother, who engages in violent outbursts against Akiyuki and his mother after she remarries and moves with Akiyuki to her new husband's house, leaving her older children behind. This half-brother commits suicide when Akiyuki is twelve, but his violence haunts Akiyuki long after his death. The specter of repetition is everywhere in "The Cape," and eventually the violence between brothers spills into the present when Yasuo, a laborer and Akiyuki's in-law, murders his own brother-in-law, Furuichi.

In addition to his anguish about his elder half-brother, Akiyuki feels himself to be an orphan, surrounded by relatives to whom he feels a tenuous connection. When Akiyuki was a child of three, his mother rejected his natural father, declaring that she would

---

[11] In fact, in its adherence to personal experience, its one-sided perspective (we view the world through Akiyuki's eyes) and its rough edges suggesting the fabric of lived experience, "The Cape" even approaches the *shishōsetsu* form, a hallowed form of confessional, pseudo-autobiographical writing that has dogged the footsteps of modern Japanese literature. The *shishōsetsu* spins what Edward Fowler calls, "a myth of sincerity," a rhetorical strategy that draws the reader into the protagonist/author's struggle and then practices a cleansing ritual of "confession" that elevates fiction above the level of mere entertainment. See Edward Fowler, *The Rhetoric of Confession* (Berkeley: University of California Press, 1988), pp. 64–70.

like to drain the father's blood from Akiyuki's body. In search of a key to the riddle of his own identity and the mystery of his blood, Akiyuki turns toward his natural father, yet this strategy merely heightens his confusion. Akiyuki's father is a suspicious drifter who appeared in the *roji* after the war, impregnated three women, including Akiyuki's mother, and then attempted to drive the people out of the *roji* by setting fires. The young boy has little contact with his father, but as he grows up he feels his father's gaze on him in town; the eyes are relentless and Akiyuki feels that he is his father's prey.

Faced with the impossibility of connections with others (his mother and siblings are suffocating him; his father hounds him but does not claim him), Akiyuki turns inward to pose the question, "Who am I?" Interestingly, his answer comes through the contemplation of landscape, as he creates a self that transcends the context of the family and defies the need for names:

> Next to the railroad crossing, where the alleyway curved off to the left, a single tree was gently shaking its leaves. The tree reminded him of himself. Akiyuki didn't know what kind of tree it was, and he didn't care. The tree had no flowers or fruit. It spread its branches to the sun, it trembled in the wind. That's enough, he thought. The tree doesn't need flowers or fruit. It doesn't need a name. Suddenly, Akiyuki felt he was dreaming. [p. 11]

The act of creation is necessarily dreamlike, for the self is not fashioned through direct conflict with others but, as Paul Anderer suggests, in carefully guarded moments of silence and retreat.[12] Yet Nakagami subtly alters the role of "nature" here, having Aki-

---

[12] Paul Anderer, *Other Worlds: Arishima Takeo and the Bounds of Modern Japanese Fiction* (New York: Columbia University Press, 1984), pp. 15–16.

yuki follow the example of the nameless tree. Rather than serve as a screen upon which Akiyuki projects his internal struggle, the tree trembles with the weight of its own life and leads Akiyuki in the dance of self-creation.

Akiyuki's dreams of transcendence, however, are fleeting; the world drags him back and he cannot escape the demand to claim a father. Each time Akiyuki passes a mirror, his own features press the claim further, showing him to be a child of "that man":

> Akiyuki's older brother had died at the age he was now. But he couldn't believe that he looked like him, as his mother and sister always said he did. Akiyuki was big. With rough hands and feet.... Akiyuki's face belonged to that man. The ugliest face in the world, the crudest face, a face full of evil. [p. 25]

Throughout the story, the women see a resemblance to Ikuo in Akiyuki's features, but to Akiyuki, caught up in the problem of identity, the mirror reflects only the "evil" face of the father.

In many modern Japanese novels, the protagonist struggles to break the hold of an authoritarian male figure, who is, he believes, the last obstacle to shaking off the past and pursuing a clear vision of the self. In "Aru Otoko" (A Man) for example, Shiga Naoya, the grandfather of auto-biographical Japanese prose fiction, mentions, "the riddle that the existence of the father poses to the son."[13] On the one hand, Akiyuki's struggle with an absent father is an ironic version of a traditional theme; the father's image taunts him but never solidifies. At the same time, however, Akiyuki cannot rid himself of the vision of his father's ugly features. The father's ugliness is deeply problematic:

---

[13] *Shiga Naoya Zenshū (Collected Works of Shiga Naoya)* 2:446, quoted in Fowler, *Rhetoric of Confession*, pp. 206–7.

it is a sign of the pain of bastard origins, a metaphor for the out-caste within the outcaste. It is further synonymous with naked sexual desire, another characteristic that is projected upon the males of the *buraku*.[14] By rejecting his own sexual coming-of-age, Akiyuki can avoid the moment of his own self-recognition and postpone his confrontation with this father. He is curious about sex, but rejects a prostitute because he is afraid of what he might become:

> The alley in the red-light district smelled faintly of sewage and piss.
> "Come here, handsome," a woman called to him. He didn't answer.
> "Stop in for a while," said the woman, now taking him by the arm. He could smell makeup and liquor. He had money. Enough money to get drunk and buy a woman. But he'd never had a woman and he didn't want one now. Didn't want to dirty himself in something pointless and messy. No, no, he worried that if he did it just once, he'd become obsessed with it and end up with his mind in the sewer just like that man, who couldn't keep his hands to himself.
> [p. 24]

As "The Cape" draws to a close, however, Akiyuki emerges from his cocoon. Repeatedly, he finds himself drawn back to the red-light district to search for one of his half-siblings, a prostitute, one of the three children fathered by "that man" after the war. Akiyuki eventually sleeps with his half-sister, and by doing so he confronts his father, declaring to himself that he and his sister are "pure" children (p. 91). Formerly a source and sign of pollution, sex has

---

[14] George De Vos and Hiroshi Wagatsuma, *Japan's Invisible Race* (Berkeley: University of California Press, 1966), pp. 139, 229.

become the means for accomplishing an inversion: Akiyuki and his half-sister break the ancient taboo against incest, purify themselves, and rise above their own suspect origins. Again, Nakagami works with mythic elements. In the creation myth of Japan, the gods Izanagi and Izanami, a "brother" and "sister" pair, create the islands of Japan through an act of sex. In "The Cape," the land (in the form of the cape) becomes a figure of sexuality itself against which Akiyuki violently creates himself, displaces the father, and makes a new world above and beyond the father's law. When Akiyuki feels the body of his sister beneath him, he visualizes himself as the cape jutting into the sea. At this moment, he possess the vitality of the land itself:

> "Do you ever think of dying?" he asked.
> "Damn, you're really hopeless," the woman said. She wrapped her feet around his. "At my age, why would I think about such things? One of these days I'm going to marry a very rich man. You musn't butt in and say I worked as a prostitute here when the time comes."
> He nodded. She reached out for his penis again. A vision came to him of the cape protruding into the sea. Swell up, rise up, he thought. Tear the sea to pieces. She took his swollen penis and began to caress it vigorously. [p. 91]

In addition to representing the dynamics of Akiyuki's desire and the mythic solution to the problem of origins, Nakagami also widens the parameters of the story through his portrayal of the cape. The cape is not only a phallic projection in Akiyuki's mind but is also the point of origin for Akiyuki's family, their burial ground, and the place where Mie, another half-sister, returns momentarily to live in the happiness of the past. The cape once served as the home of Akiyuki's people, the outcastes of Kishū, who lived there in grinding poverty and did not have access to the riches of the sea. The cape epitomizes the tenacity of the outcastes who survive even at the ends of the land, and who, imbued with the vigor of sexuality itself, continually remind the majority of their existence. In *Kishū Ki no Kuni Ne no Kuni* (Kishū: Land of Trees and Roots), a non-fictional account of a journey around the Kii Peninsula, Nakagami describes what he calls the "peninsula condition":

> As is true everywhere, a peninsula is a place that has been fed table scraps and treated like a parasite....As I traveled through Kishū along the Kii Peninsula, I thought about the meaning of the peninsula....The peninsula lies between the legs of the continent, the shameful protrusion of the mountains and the plains. Consider it a piece of shame, shameful because it's nature that can't be beaten down, a metaphor for sex. Yet as I traveled the peninsula, I realized that the peninsula is not a metaphor for sex—it's sex itself.[15]

Read in this light, "The Cape" is more than the story of a young man coming of age. It is Nakagami's attempt to dramatically revise the boundaries of modern Japanese fiction by expanding the story of one young man's sexual awakening to represent the story of a people. Sex—without the intervention of metaphor—becomes a testimony not only to survival and the perpetuation of life, but also to the continuation of a binding communal identity. Rather than reduce landscape to a reflection of the pro-

---

[15] Nakagami Kenji, *Kishū: Ki no Kuni Ne no Kuni (Kishū: Land of Trees and Roots)* (Tokyo: Kadokawa Shoten, 1986), p. 7.

tagonist's consciousness, landscape creates both Akiyuki and his people, linking them through a specific and deeply rooted history of oppression. In "The Cape" Nakagami begins where other many other Japanese writers do—with the problem of anxiety over one's origins, but he then widens the scope of his work using landscape to illuminate the problem of outcaste identity.

House on Fire

Written a few months before "The Cape" and published in 1975, "House on Fire," is a structurally complex tale that moves back and forth in time between different characters and perspectives. The story is framed around the bastard son of an arsonist who hears that his father is in a hospital bed, his body shattered in a motorcycle accident. After the news of the accident, the grown son tries to sort out his own relationship to his natural father by reconstructing the experiences of an older brother who doggedly followed the man from fire to fire and later committed suicide. At times the son's own few memories of childhood intrude into the narrative as do events from his present life as he tries to piece together an identity from memories, fragments, and family history.

The characters in "House on Fire" are earlier versions of Akiyuki and his family in "The Cape." Nakagami moves backward in time to the moment before Akiyuki's birth in order to address a central question: If the father is an arsonist, will the baby in the belly be one, too? "House on Fire" is an exercise in the exploration of identity, but because the events of the narrative occur at such a remove from the protagonist, the past also attains the status of myth. By filtering family history through the reconstructed memories of the and downward, they lack the power to project violence where it might in fact prove destabilizing. In "House on Fire" Nakagami problematizes violence, first challenging the status quo through the portrayal of a father who burns his way through the world and then sinking into the quagmire of the son's self-contemplation. The violent spectacle becomes private, limited, lacking the collective impulse to confront the conditions of one's own oppression—whether self-imposed or otherwise. After the son's rampage, we awake to find that the world has not changed: the glass of the chandelier has been swept away, the violent spectacle serving merely as a private declaration of one's own existence.

In fact, Nakagami himself recognized the self-referential nature of the violent outburst and its tendency to replicate the very forces that give rise to it. He makes this point, not surprisingly, through the figure of the wife. The wife clearly recognizes that what begins as a form of anarchy (the flames sweeping out of control) ends in *sabetsu* or "discrimination"—the making of differences and the reassertion of hierarchies. She points out the error (and the tyranny) of the son's position:

"You think people are insects, don't you, and you're the only human being in the world, but tell me, what is the difference between you and me? Just try and tell me. Give me one reason why a man should beat up a woman." [p. 133]

It is here that Nakagami illustrates the trap of subjectivity: the son will never transcend his own frame of reference but will continue to pursue violence for its utopian promise and the hope of transforming himself into the father. Still, Nakagami refuses to censor the violent impulses of his protagonists, and this refusal reveals his own ambivalent relationship to violence. Through violence, Nakagami expresses his disgust with the proj-

dead brother, the story unfolds in a golden time before the history of Akiyuki begins.

The mythic element of "House on Fire" is realized most thoroughly in the characterization of the father, who embodies a perfect and primitive form of violence. Like the fires he sets, the pure heat of the man's violence destroys everything in its path. The father himself is mesmerized by the force of the annihilation that he has unleashed:

He could hear the man's voice calling his brother. The flames rose. Each time they did, a voice called out in the crowd. The man could feel the brother staring at him. Fire puts people in a trance. The man patted the brother's head. I'm the one who released the flames, but the instant fire leaves my hand, it moves of its own accord and devours everything in its path.... [p. 134]

In the father's hands, violence has the force to undo a community, to take the mother hostage, or in the words of Karatani Kōjin, to "affirm the here and now," which he defines as "transformation, variation, and the dissolution of the categories of good and evil."[16]

The "house on fire" in the story's title refers to any number of edifices on fire: the son's house in the present, the mother's house—the "nest" where she gives birth—the homes of the outcaste families who are victims of the man's schemes, even the sacred institution of the Japanese *ie*, or family line. Nakagami inverts the image of the patriarch who represents order and

[16] Karatani Kōjin, *Hihyō to Posuto-modan (Criticism and the Postmodern)* (Tokyo: Fukutake Shoten, 1980), p. 85. Also see Steve Dodd on the liberating force of fire in the story, in "Japan's Private Parts: Place as Metaphor in Nakagami Kenji's Works," Japan Forum 8:1 (1996), p. 10.

authority—this father sets fires—much in the same way that Ōe Kenzaburō creates a perverse picture of a fat father rotting to death in his darkened storehouse in "Warera no Kyōki o Ikino-biru Michi o Oshieyo" (Teach Us to Outgrow Our Madness).

The operations of violence are perfectly illustrated in the cock-fighting scene where one bird kills another and human violence is forestalled for a time. In the ring, the fight takes the form of a sacri-ficial ritual stimulating and satiating bloodlust; violence erupts in a shower of blood but is contained in the ring where the birds prevent the men from turning their knives on each other. Interestingly, the father's world, situated at the very bottom of the social ladder, forms another sort of ring, a limbo where violence both explodes and is contained. In his many fights, for example, the father knows that the force of the blow speaks for itself and that there is no need for reflection.

Once violence enters the son's realm, however, it becomes mud-died. To the son, violence cannot simply be a force of anarchy or presentness; it is saturated with meaning because it holds the key to his own identity. In fact, violence submits to narrative—it is forced to give itself up to legibility—because the son seeks to imprint meaning upon random events as he pieces together the story of his life. Rather than create an eternal present, violence exhibits its own peculiar logic, its own singular patterns that shape the telling of the tale.

In "House on Fire" violence seems to unite father and son. The one clear memory that the son has of the father is during a fight between the father and another man at a school fair. Watching the father knock down his opponent without uttering a word, the boy feels "something stirring and rising within him." Violence is a wordless stream that passes between them and the symbol of a paternal legacy.

The violence of the father mesmerizes the son, who suspects

its link to sexuality—to what it means to become a man—but the son never achieves the white heat of the father's violence. In adulthood, the son's violence is petty and sordid, played out in a claustrophobic domestic sphere. He turns on his tired wife in her dressing gown and the props of middle-class life, the refrigerator full of food and the glass chandelier. Yet there is nothing comic about this scene; rather, the son cannot attain the purity of the impulse represented by the father. He can only approximate an ideal.

The gap between the father's mythic violence and the petty bullying of the son reveals the tragedy of the son's position: he is caught up in the riddle of his own identity. Rather than sim-ply exist, he is forced to contemplate, the task of any good pro-tagonist in fiction. But the son finds that nothing fits: he longs to be "a good person" (p. 131) but hits his wife and alienates his children. He remembers how he loved the man but was forced to reject him at the age of three. Thinking of these contradictions, the son's mind is flooded with ambiguities that cannot be toler-ated, except by eruptions of further violence. In the hands of the son, violence is a feeble attempt to shore up a vital piece of him-self that has cracked or broken away.[17]

Perhaps the central problem of Nakagami's fiction is that his pro-tagonists are not violent enough. Turning the force of violence inward

[17] The subject of male-on-female violence in Nakagami's work has generated significant controversy in Japanese literary circles. At a 1993 symposium, for example, when I raised the subject, Watanabe Naomi expressed the view that violence toward women in Nakagami's fiction is a literary strategy, a means of assaulting the traditional tale that is associated with the female (*Bungakkai*, October 1993). Other critics react strongly to any mention of this issue, dismissing the topic by pointing to scenes in which women lead men to bed or to bisexual imagery. For a detailed discussion of violence and gender in Nakagami's work see Livia Monnet, "Ghostly Women, Displaced Femininities and Male Family Romances: Violence, Gender and Sexuality in Two Texts by Nakagami Kenji," *Japan Forum* 8.1 (1996), pp. 13–34.

ect of modern Japanese fiction—the refining and propagation of the self. But he also exhibits a deep fascination with the forms of violence, a desire for a mythic catharsis that will never be, and a longing for the father who runs "as though his feet had wings" (p. 107).

Red Hair

"Red Hair" is a seemingly effortless piece of fiction; it moves forward from one day to the next, creating a kind of real fictional time and allowing very little to ripple its dispassionate surface.[18] Kōzō, the protagonist, goes to work and comes home again to make love to a woman with red hair. There are undercurrents, however, events and images that root the story in the 1970s and suggest that the world outside Kōzō's room is changing. Kōzō himself is gradually being dislocated by bosses who organize their workers into cartels and by machines that do his job in a fraction of the time. Sex becomes an antidote: when Kōzō hears that there is no work to be had one day, he fantasizes about sex with the woman, recalling "the woman's tongue tirelessly licking his tired cock that would ache when it grew erect" (p. 145). At least there is one outlet for Kōzō's excess energy.

Behind the use of sex as an antidote, however, there are darker undertones to "Red Hair" suggesting an affinity with Imamura

---

[18] Like "The Cape," "Red Hair" perpetuates Nakagami's image as an anti-intellectual. In an essay published in 1978 shortly after the story appeared in print, Sasaki Yukitsuna discovers no social or political implications to Nakagami's story but simply notes "the harmonious feeling human beings get when they experience themselves as a part of nature." *Shunkan Dokushojin*, 8 May 1978.

Shōhei's 1979 film *Fukushū Suruwa Ware ni Ari* (Vengeance Is Mine), a tale about a rootless, oversexed drifter who revels in disguises and who murders strangers and lovers with great aplomb.[19] In "Red Hair," moments of ecstasy are punctuated by the screams of another young woman who lives in the same complex, an addict who loses control nightly under the influence of speed. The redhead lies awake listening to the agonized wails of the woman "as if they were the refrain of her new life." Further dark images abound: the drowned body of the woman's friend, speckled with needle marks; the magazine story that Kōzō and his friends read about a man who heightens sexual pleasure by strangling his lovers; Kōzō's threat to rip the woman's womb in two for the sake of his own pleasure. As in Imamura's film, the search for pleasure involves taking hostages and exerting control over a limited environment when the world outside is beyond one's control.

The darker moments of the story hint at a murderous climax, but unlike much of Nakagami's other fiction and Imamura's film, there is no apocalypse. Nakagami surprises us. The story ends where it begins—with the woman's red hair. Represented by her hair, a sign of her sexual prowess and experience, the woman is simply the sum of body parts: a small breast that fits into Kōzō's palm, black nipples, a tongue, lips, hands, knees, crotch, toes. Kōzō, too, is fragmented: watching himself in the mirror, he sees himself as a collection of substances (semen, sweat, and saliva) for the woman's consumption. Through a continual exchange of scents, fluids, and genitals, Nakagami experiments with a wholly physical form of subjectivity—Kōzō is a man who knows himself through the body of another.

With nowhere to go, the narrative, too, meanders with little

---

[19] I was introduced to this film by Dennis Washburn, "Reading Practices" Seminar, Edwin O. Reischauer Institute of Japanese Studies, Harvard University, May 1998.

attention to plan. In fact there is very little story: Kōzō shows
no interest in the woman's past or future and is simply content to
hold on to her warm body. We never discover the true identity
of the woman, nor are we made to care about her past. The story
is simply the sum of its repetitive caresses, its many climaxes.
Interestingly, it is the woman who finally recognizes the utopian
quality of the lovers' withdrawal from the world. Looking out the
window at the rain one morning, she suggests that they go back
to bed because they cannot hold off the world forever: "It's not
always going to rain like this," she tells Kōzō (p. 164). But for a
few days at least Kōzō and the woman hold on to the illusion of
the moment, shedding their clothes over and over and celebrating
the rhythms of sex.

After the complex genealogy and the struggle between father
and son so painstakingly detailed in "House on Fire" and "The
Cape," "Red Hair" shows Nakagami moving off in different
directions, experimenting with less weighty forms of subjectivity.
Perhaps more than any other Nakagami protagonist, Kōzō stands
simply for the body. But Akiyuki with his dreams of nature and
the son with his longing for a perfect kind of violence also show
the versatility of Nakagami, a writer who reveled in experimentation and variation even as he struggled to create literary language
anew. As the incoming tide alters the line of the beach, Nakagami transformed modern Japanese fiction—decoding Japanese
myth, posing complex questions about violence and identity, and
reconfiguring the position of the hero.

Biographical Note

Nakagami Kenji was born in the outcaste neighborhood of Shingū, Wakayama, in August 1946, the product of an affair his mother had with a man from Arima. In 1954, his mother moved in with Nakaue Shichirō, her second husband. Five years later, Nakagami's older half-brother, Ikuhei, committed suicide at the old family house.

Around this time Kenji began to use his stepfather's name, Nakaue, which transforms into "Nakagami" (a different reading of the same characters) when he goes to Tokyo, where he promised his family he would study for the entrance exams to Waseda University. Instead of studying, Nakagami wrote poetry, spent his days at Jazz Village, a jazz bar in Shinjuku, and moved around Tokyo from one tiny apartment to the next depending on an allowance from home. By 1965, Nakagami was publishing poems in small magazines.

Nakagami married Yamaguchi Kasumi, a fellow writer, in 1970. By the early and mid-seventies he was devoting more time to fiction, and his name began to appear in the better literary magazines. The three stories in this volume date from this period. In January 1976 "Misaki" won the 74th Akutagawa Prize for literature, Nakagami's first rite of passage as a writer.

Over the next ten years or so Nakagami would write long works of fiction—*Karekinada* (Withered Tree Straits) and *Chi no Hate Shijō no Toki* (The Sublime Time at the Ends of the Earth), the sequels to "The Cape," and *Sennen no Yuraku* (A Thousand Years of Pleasure)—plus numerous collections of "mythic" tales, including *Kumano-shū* (A Kumano Collection) and *Juryoku no Miyako* (The City of Gravity).

In the latter half of the 1980s Nakagami's literary output slowed briefly while he traveled extensively (he spent a semester at Columbia University) and branched out in his literary pursuits. By the late 1980s, he was back at work writing book-length new fiction: *Kiseki* (Miracle, 1989), *Sanka* (Hymn, 1990), *Keibetsu* (Scorn, 1992), and *Izoku* (The Tribe), a long, unfinished novel.

Early in 1992, Nakagami learned he had kidney cancer. In July 1992, he returned to his family home in Shingū with his wife and died there, not long after his forty-sixth birthday, on August 12.

authority—this father sets fires—much in the same way that Ōe Kenzaburō creates a perverse picture of a fat father rotting to death in his darkened storehouse in "Warera no Kyōki o Ikino-biru Michi o Oshieyo" (Teach Us to Outgrow Our Madness).

The operations of violence are perfectly illustrated in the cock-fighting scene where one bird kills another and human violence is forestalled for a time. In the ring, the fight takes the form of a sacrificial ritual stimulating and satiating bloodlust; violence erupts in a shower of blood but is contained in the ring where the birds prevent the men from turning their knives on each other. Interestingly, the father's world, situated at the very bottom of the social ladder, forms another sort of ring, a limbo where violence both explodes and is contained. In his many fights, for example, the father knows that the force of the blow speaks for itself and that there is no need for reflection.

Once violence enters the son's realm, however, it becomes muddied. To the son, violence cannot simply be a force of anarchy or presentness; it is saturated with meaning because it holds the key to his own identity. In fact, violence submits to narrative—it is forced to give itself up to legibility—because the son seeks to imprint meaning upon random events as he pieces together the story of his life. Rather than create an eternal present, violence exhibits its own peculiar logic, its own singular patterns that shape the telling of the tale.

In "House on Fire" violence seems to unite father and son. The one clear memory that the son has of the father is during a fight between the father and another man at a school fair. Watching the father knock down his opponent without uttering a word, the boy feels "something stirring and rising within him." Violence is a wordless stream that passes between them and the symbol of a paternal legacy.

The violence of the father mesmerizes the son, who suspects

dead brother, the story unfolds in a golden time before the history of Akiyuki begins.

The mythic element of "House on Fire" is realized most thoroughly in the characterization of the father, who embodies a perfect and primitive form of violence. Like the fires he sets, the pure heat of the man's violence destroys everything in its path. The father himself is mesmerized by the force of the annihilation that he has unleashed:

> He could hear the man's voice calling his brother. The flames rose. Each time they did, a voice called out in the crowd. The man could feel the brother staring at him. Fire puts people in a trance. The man patted the brother's head. I'm the one who released the flames, but the instant fire leaves my hand, it moves of its own accord and devours everything in its path.... [p. 134]

In the father's hands, violence has the force to undo a community, to take the mother hostage, or in the words of Karatani Kōjin, to "affirm the here and now," which he defines as "transformation, variation, and the dissolution of the categories of good and evil."[16]

The "house on fire" in the story's title refers to any number of edifices on fire: the son's house in the present, the mother's house—the "nest" where she gives birth—the homes of the outcaste families who are victims of the man's schemes, even the sacred institution of the Japanese *ie*, or family line. Nakagami inverts the image of the patriarch who represents order and

---

[16] Karatani Kōjin, *Hihyō to Posuto-modan (Criticism and the Postmodern)* (Tokyo: Fukutake Shoten, 1980), p. 85. Also see Steve Dodd on the liberating force of fire in the story, in "Japan's Private Parts: Place as Metaphor in Nakagami Kenji's Works," Japan Forum 8:1 (1996), p. 10.

its link to sexuality—to what it means to become a man—but the son never achieves the white heat of the father's violence. In adulthood, the son's violence is petty and sordid, played out in a claustrophobic domestic sphere. He turns on his tired wife in her dressing gown and the props of middle-class life, the refrigerator full of food and the glass chandelier. Yet there is nothing comic about this scene; rather, the son cannot attain the purity of the impulse represented by the father. He can only approximate an ideal.

The gap between the father's mythic violence and the petty bullying of the son reveals the tragedy of the son's position: he is caught up in the riddle of his own identity. Rather than simply exist, he is forced to contemplate, the task of any good protagonist in fiction. But the son finds that nothing fits: he longs to be "a good person" (p. 131) but hits his wife and alienates his children. He remembers how he loved the man but was forced to reject him at the age of three. Thinking of these contradictions, the son's mind is flooded with ambiguities that cannot be tolerated, except by eruptions of further violence. In the hands of the son, violence is a feeble attempt to shore up a vital piece of himself that has cracked or broken away.[17]

Perhaps the central problem of Nakagami's fiction is that his protagonists are not violent enough. Turning the force of violence inward

---

[17] The subject of male-on-female violence in Nakagami's work has generated significant controversy in Japanese literary circles. At a 1993 symposium, for example, when I raised the subject, Watanabe Naomi expressed the view that violence toward women in Nakagami's fiction is a literary strategy, a means of assaulting the traditional tale that is associated with the female (*Bungakkai*, October 1993). Other critics react strongly to any mention of this issue, dismissing the topic by pointing to scenes in which women lead men to bed or to bisexual imagery. For a detailed discussion of violence and gender in Nakagami's work see Livia Monnet, "Ghostly Women, Displaced Femininities and Male Family Romances: Violence, Gender and Sexuality in Two Texts by Nakagami Kenji," *Japan Forum* 8.1 (1996), pp. 13–34.

and downward, they lack the power to project violence where it might in fact prove destabilizing. In "House on Fire" Nakagami problematizes violence, first challenging the status quo through the portrayal of a father who burns his way through the world and then sinking into the quagmire of the son's self-contemplation. The violent spectacle becomes private, limited, lacking the collective impulse to confront the conditions of one's own oppression—whether self-imposed or otherwise. After the son's rampage, we awake to find that the world has not changed: the glass of the chandelier has been swept away, the violent spectacle serving merely as a private declaration of one's own existence.

In fact, Nakagami himself recognized the self-referential nature of the violent outburst and its tendency to replicate the very forces that give rise to it. He makes this point, not surprisingly, through the figure of the wife. The wife clearly recognizes that what begins as a form of anarchy (the flames sweeping out of control) ends in *sabetsu* or "discrimination"—the making of differences and the reassertion of hierarchies. She points out the error (and the tyranny) of the son's position:

> "You think people are insects, don't you, and you're the only human being in the world, but tell me, what is the difference between you and me? Just try and tell me. Give me one reason why a man should beat up a woman." [p. 133]

It is here that Nakagami illustrates the trap of subjectivity: the son will never transcend his own frame of reference but will continue to pursue violence for its utopian promise and the hope of transforming himself into the father. Still, Nakagami refuses to censor the violent impulses of his protagonists, and this refusal reveals his own ambivalent relationship to violence. Through violence, Nakagami expresses his disgust with the proj-

ect of modern Japanese fiction—the refining and propagation of
the self. But he also exhibits a deep fascination with the forms of
violence, a desire for a mythic catharsis that will never be, and a
longing for the father who runs "as though his feet had wings"
(p. 107).

Red Hair

"Red Hair" is a seemingly effortless piece of fiction; it moves forward from one day to the next, creating a kind of real fictional
time and allowing very little to ripple its dispassionate surface.[18]
Kōzō, the protagonist, goes to work and comes home again to
make love to a woman with red hair. There are undercurrents,
however, events and images that root the story in the 1970s and
suggest that the world outside Kōzō's room is changing. Kōzō
himself is gradually being dislocated by bosses who organize
their workers into cartels and by machines that do his job in a
fraction of the time. Sex becomes an antidote: when Kōzō hears
that there is no work to be had one day, he fantasizes about sex
with the woman, recalling "the woman's tongue tirelessly licking
his tired cock that would ache when it grew erect" (p. 145). At
least there is one outlet for Kōzō's excess energy.

Behind the use of sex as an antidote, however, there are darker
undertones to "Red Hair" suggesting an affinity with Imamura

---

[18] Like "The Cape," "Red Hair" perpetuates Nakagami's image as an anti-intellectual. In an essay published in 1978 shortly after the story appeared in print,
Sasaki Yukitsuna discovers no social or political implications to Nakagami's
story but simply notes "the harmonious feeling human beings get when they
experience themselves as a part of nature." *Shunkan Dokushojin*, 8 May 1978.

Shōhei's 1979 film *Fukushū Suruwa Ware ni Ari* (Vengeance Is Mine), a tale about a rootless, oversexed drifter who revels in disguises and who murders strangers and lovers with great aplomb.[19] In "Red Hair," moments of ecstasy are punctuated by the screams of another young woman who lives in the same complex, an addict who loses control nightly under the influence of speed. The redhead lies awake listening to the agonized wails of the woman "as if they were the refrain of her new life." Further dark images abound: the drowned body of the woman's friend, speckled with needle marks; the magazine story that Kōzō and his friends read about a man who heightens sexual pleasure by strangling his lovers; Kōzō's threat to rip the woman's womb in two for the sake of his own pleasure. As in Imamura's film, the search for pleasure involves taking hostages and exerting control over a limited environment when the world outside is beyond one's control.

The darker moments of the story hint at a murderous climax, but unlike much of Nakagami's other fiction and Imamura's film, there is no apocalypse. Nakagami surprises us. The story ends where it begins—with the woman's red hair. Represented by her hair, a sign of her sexual prowess and experience, the woman is simply the sum of body parts: a small breast that fits into Kōzō's palm, black nipples, a tongue, lips, hands, knees, crotch, toes. Kōzō, too, is fragmented: watching himself in the mirror, he sees himself as a collection of substances (semen, sweat, and saliva) for the woman's consumption. Through a continual exchange of scents, fluids, and genitals, Nakagami experiments with a wholly physical form of subjectivity—Kōzō is a man who knows himself through the body of another.

With nowhere to go, the narrative, too, meanders with little

---

[19] I was introduced to this film by Dennis Washburn, "Reading Practices" Seminar, Edwin O. Reischauer Institute of Japanese Studies, Harvard University, May 1998.

attention to plan. In fact there is very little story: Kōzō shows no interest in the woman's past or future and is simply content to hold on to her warm body. We never discover the true identity of the woman, nor are we made to care about her past. The story is simply the sum of its repetitive caresses, its many climaxes. Interestingly, it is the woman who finally recognizes the utopian quality of the lovers' withdrawal from the world. Looking out the window at the rain one morning, she suggests that they go back to bed because they cannot hold off the world forever: "It's not always going to rain like this," she tells Kōzō (p. 164). But for a few days at least Kōzō and the woman hold on to the illusion of the moment, shedding their clothes over and over and celebrating the rhythms of sex.

After the complex genealogy and the struggle between father and son so painstakingly detailed in "House on Fire" and "The Cape," "Red Hair" shows Nakagami moving off in different directions, experimenting with less weighty forms of subjectivity. Perhaps more than any other Nakagami protagonist, Kōzō stands simply for the body. But Akiyuki with his dreams of nature and the son with his longing for a perfect kind of violence also show the versatility of Nakagami, a writer who reveled in experimentation and variation even as he struggled to create literary language anew. As the incoming tide alters the line of the beach, Nakagami transformed modern Japanese fiction—decoding Japanese myth, posing complex questions about violence and identity, and reconfiguring the position of the hero.

Biographical Note

Nakagami Kenji was born in the outcaste neighborhood of Shingū, Wakayama, in August 1946, the product of an affair his mother had with a man from Arima. In 1954, his mother moved in with Nakaue Shichirō, her second husband. Five years later, Nakagami's older half-brother, Ikuhei, committed suicide at the old family house.

Around this time Kenji began to use his stepfather's name, Nakaue, which transforms into "Nakagami" (a different reading of the same characters) when he goes to Tokyo, where he promised his family he would study for the entrance exams to Waseda University. Instead of studying, Nakagami wrote poetry, spent his days at Jazz Village, a jazz bar in Shinjuku, and moved around Tokyo from one tiny apartment to the next depending on an allowance from home. By 1965, Nakagami was publishing poems in small magazines.

Nakagami married Yamaguchi Kasumi, a fellow writer, in 1970. By the early and mid-seventies he was devoting more time to fiction, and his name began to appear in the better literary magazines. The three stories in this volume date from this period. In January 1976 "Misaki" won the 74th Akutagawa Prize for literature, Nakagami's first rite of passage as a writer.

Over the next ten years or so Nakagami would write long works of fiction—*Karekinada* (Withered Tree Straits) and *Chi no Hate Shijō no Toki* (The Sublime Time at the Ends of the Earth), the sequels to "The Cape," and *Sennen no Yuraku* (A Thousand Years of Pleasure)—plus numerous collections of "mythic" tales, including *Kumano-shū* (A Kumano Collection) and *Juryoku no Miyako* (The City of Gravity).

In the latter half of the 1980s Nakagami's literary output slowed briefly while he traveled extensively (he spent a semester at Columbia University) and branched out in his literary pursuits. By the late 1980s, he was back at work writing book-length new fiction: *Kiseki* (Miracle, 1989), *Sanka* (Hymn, 1990), *Keibetsu* (Scorn, 1992), and *Izoku* (The Tribe), a long, unfinished novel.

Early in 1992, Nakagami learned he had kidney cancer. In July 1992, he returned to his family home in Shingū with his wife and died there, not long after his forty-sixth birthday, on August 12.